The
Francie LeVillard
Mysteries

Volume One

The
Francie LeVillard
Mysteries

Volume One

by Tony Seton

Carmel, California
March 2013

These stories are pure fiction – ideas snatched from head-lines and whole cloth – and massaged by imagination and driven fingers. There is no correlation to either real people or events, at least none that you would recognize..

The Francie LeVillard Mysteries
Volume One

ISBN-10: 1466372060
ISBN-13: 978-1466372061

Printed in the United States of America

Table of Contents

Thank You

To the late Jim Cardwell, Dr. Stancil Johnson, the Diogenes Club of Carmel-by-the Sea, and Sir Arthur Conan Doyle;

To Denise Swenson and Michelle Manos for their etymological attention to this manuscript;

To Ginger Coffee for her friendship.

The Francie LeVillard Mysteries

Introduction

I've been a fan of Sherlock Holmes from my early youth. That appreciation ratcheted up a notch in the winter of 1986 when I was first invited by a new friend, Jim Cardwell, to attend a Sherlock Holmes society dinner. I had met Jim when he hired me to teach a course in *Documentary Film Writing* at Monterey Peninsula College. "Adobe James" was a prolific writer himself, having penned hundreds of short stories, some of which had been picked up by Hollywood.

The dinner of the Diogenes Club of Carmel-by-the-Sea was a black-tie affair held that night at the Monterey Plaza Hotel. I was pleased to meet a number of other similarly-minded gentlemen, some who are still friends today. Upon my third guest visit, I was invited to deliver a paper on a Holmesian topic – I spoke of Sir Arthur Conan Doyle's brilliance as a writer – and was then proudly inducted into the Diogenes Club. My investiture name – we all took names from the Canon – was François Le Villard, a star detective with the Deuxième Bureau in Paris who had worked with Holmes.

It was during the following January that the lady who was sharing a house with me on the south end of Carmel Bay decided that she needed a breather from me and she went north to Sonoma County to be with family. Alone, and loving it, I took up the pen to write poetry, something I hadn't done since prep school. The first poem, titled "Barefoot Gypsy Rage," was published by the *Monterey Peninsula Herald*. They paid me seven dollars.

More to the point, I shifted the genre and started writing detective stories featuring Francie LeVillard, a female consulting detective ala Sherlock Holmes. Well, not really so like him, as you shall see. I wrote six short stories in two weeks.

And then I put them aside...for twenty years...until she stepped through a curtain in my mind, like Holmes escaping Reichenbach Falls, and I started writing her stories again. She has certainly demanded my attention and compliance. I wound up writing twenty more stories featuring this extraordinary woman.

On December 1st 2011, I began posting the new stories online, episodically on the first and fifteen of the month. I didn't publish the whole of each story. I kept back the side story so that when I would publish volumes of *The Francie LeVillard Mysteries,* there would be good reason for those millions of avid online readers to peruse the books. And to be clear, the side stories are quite worthwhile.

Volume One features three of the stories that were produced online, but here they are complete. There is also a dramatic play presented on March 10th 2013 in Monterey as a fundraiser for the Friends of the Symphony.

If you enjoy what you read, make room on your library shelves, as I am expecting to publish three more volumes this year. That's the plan, at least.

Thank you for your interest.

Tony Seton
Carmel-by-the-Sea
March 2013

Meet Francie LeVillard

Francie (Francine) LeVillard is the great-granddaughter of François Le Villard, the renowned detective who was with the Deuxième Bureau in Paris and who worked closely with Sherlock Holmes a century earlier.

Francie got her professional investigative start, working in television news on the East Coast. But after ten years in The News Biz, picking up a number of prestigious awards along the way, Francie decided that she'd had enough of the style-over-substance approach that turned the news into the media. Especially after an ugly confrontation with the news director of her last station in Baghdad by the Bay.

She had gotten a taste of the Monterey Peninsula while working in San Francisco, and it was enough to convince her that she wanted to live on California's Central Coast. It was there, she knew, that she would find her future path.

So she moved into a small house on a bluff overlooking the Pacific, just south of the Carmel Highlands. Her first weeks were spent settling into her new home – making it her own – and exploring her new community on the Monterey Peninsula. She resumed her aikido training at the local *dojo*, took long walks by the ocean, shopped at farmers' markets every week, and played in the kitchen.

While she kept up on the news, her focus now was mostly local, as she learned about the who's and what's of her new home base. She also thought that she would made a dent in the towering pile of must-read books that had grown over the years.

But in no time at all, the genes of her forebear kicked in, and she found herself engrossed in a number of important cases. It had never been her intention, but she wound up (proverbially) hoisting above her door a shingle reading "Consulting Detective." It's how life works.

So you can more easily follow these stories, Francie describes herself thusly: "I look like I'm pushing forty if you look around my eyes. What I've seen has left its mark. Otherwise, I'm a very healthy looking specimen, five-seven and 135 pounds, a lot of it muscle because I train in aikido three times a week, and I eat healthily. I have a figure that men appreciate but I don't flaunt it. I have great legs, unless they're supposed to be long; they're great for moving quickly but not for marathons.

"My jeans aren't tight and on top I usually wear a workshirt. When I go out socially or to meet clients or interview grown-ups, I'll wear something clean and quiet but attractive. None of this short skirt nonsense that makes sitting down a challenge. Atop the clothes, whatever they be, is a slightly oval face with a light tan – my friend Ariane Chevasse says I have Basque coloring – and my straight dark hair is cut on the short side; so it doesn't block my vision.

"Oh, and one more thing about my attire but not my appearance: I carry a gun. If it's everyday with nothing on the agenda, it's a seven-shot Kel-Tec P32 which I can carry in a pocket since it's small. If I think there might be trouble, I have a .357 S&W with a 10-shot clip in a holster on the back of my belt, under a coat long enough to hide it."

A friend summed up Francie LeVillard as "attractive, bright, and bad news for bad guys."

Doc's Drugs Problem

"Is this Mrs. Villerd?" asked the voice on the phone.

Francie LeVillard had her on speaker because she'd been on hold for twenty-three minutes according to the display. She didn't do her the courtesy of picking up the handset but merely leaned forward on her folded arms and replied, emphasizing the French roots of the name, "LeVillard, and I'm not a missus."

"Oh, I'm sorry, I'm sure. Miz Villard."

Francie let the "Le" go. The woman at the other end of the call had.

"And what can I do for you today?"

"I'm following up on an email I sent to customer support last week that I didn't get a response to." Francie hated ending a sentence with a preposition, but she wanted to speak in a way that she might be understand most easily, so that she could finish this business. Little did she know. She read the woman her frequent flyer account number. "Does my email show up in your file?"

"I'm looking now..."

Francie could her the sounds of other LuxAir customer service representatives in the background. She supposed she could take some comfort from the fact that she wasn't alone in needing assistance, but in this day and age, the need for such comfort was too common, and the comfort too thin.

"I don't see it here, Miss Villard," she said. "Our computers have been running kind of slow today."

Francie might have commented that her email should have been in her file a week ago, but knew that wouldn't have moved them forward in the conversation even a millimeter.

"Then let me tell you the story quickly. I flew from Monterey to Boston last month. I used my miles to upgrade to business class. But when I got to the airport, they said there were no seats left up front so they were putting me in coach. When I got back from my trip, I checked my account and you had not restored the miles that had been taken out for the upgrade. So I wrote to customer service asking that the miles be put back. It actually happened on both the outgoing and the return, so it was fifty thousand miles that should have been put back into my account."

There was silence on the other end of the line. Practicing patience, Francie waited another twenty seconds by the clock on her computer screen and then asked, "Do you see it there in your records?"

"What?"

She resisted the urge to say "What what?" and asked her simply if she might be looking at her flight information and the negation of the use of her miles.

"When did you make the trip?"

That answered her question. Francie gave her the dates and then, keeping her tone even, she asked, "Don't you have my account there on your screen?"

"I don't have nothing on my screen," the woman said,

letting her own frustration sound in her voice. "I told you, it's being very slow today."

Francie bit her tongue. "Should I call back another time?"

"Okay," the woman replied, and then she asked, "Is there anything else I can help you with today?"

Francie had the feeling she was in a Monty Python skit. "Uh, no, I don't think so."

"Okay then, thank you for calling LuxAir."

Francie hung up the phone and said to it, "Who else would I have called?" Maybe an attorney, she thought, and walked to the kitchen to brew a cup of tea.

*   *   *   *   *

It wasn't a dark and stormy night. It was a typical grey Carmel morning. The fog sat on the ground with no apparent intention to leave. Maybe Old Sol would have shown himself late in the afternoon before he slipped behind the behemoth marine layer of more greyness that was heading toward shore from the Pacific horizon, but few would notice and fewer would be impressed.

The fog was the least of her worries; she being Francie LeVillard, the world's foremost consulting detective since the passing of Sherlock Holmes a century earlier. There weren't a lot of women in this profession, and with good reason. Maybe they were put off by the fact that detective work traditionally lent itself to a male mind, or maybe because it could get tough at times, and most women had more than enough tough in their lives. Francie had never been traditional.

Francie, from Francine, was the great-granddaughter of François Le Villard, whom Holmes readers would remember was a detective in the Deuxième Bureau in Paris, and who worked with Holmes on at least one case that was documented. Francie not only inherited his name – albeit losing the space between the two words of the last name – but also his genes. She had been a television news reporter in New York and Washington, D.C., before she found her true home south of the Carmel Highlands and took up solving problems one-on-one. Hey, journalists – the good ones – are all about investigating and finding the truth, and that's what Francie did as a detective.

So you might picture her in your mind as this story unfolds, Francie was pushing forty and looked it around her eyes. She was in good shape because she trained in aikido three times a week and spent hours walking by the Pacific; both were good for the soul as well as the body. Almost five-seven, she tipped the scale at 135 because of the muscle. She wore her dark hair short, framing an oval-ish face with Basque-ish coloring, as her friend Ariane Chevasse described it. She was certainly attractive, but she didn't make it a highlight. While she appreciated being noticed, she wanted to be seen for who she was as a person, for her character. It always gets light in the morning.

It was one recent morning, as she was leaving the post office, that a friend stopped her as she was getting into her car and asked her if she would meet privately with someone who needed help. Francie didn't know it at the time but would soon find out that it had to do with a problem that had become epidemic in this country – the theft of prescription drugs from doctors' offices. The explosion in legal pharmaceuticals produced a concomitant explosion in users – called patients in polite society – and millions of them then became addicts. Willie Sutton said he held up banks because that was where the money was. Now people were stealing from doctors and pharmacies because that was where the drugs were.

The Central Coast of California is marvelously unique in many ways, but it is not immune from the plague of drug-hungry criminals willing to ruin the lives of others along with their own. It got up close and personal for Francie when she met with that someone who needed help. That person was "Doc" Hardwicke. (His real name was Hurlbut but he hadn't used it except on government documents since even his oldest patients could remember.)

Doc was also Congressman Hardwicke. He had jumped into a Quixotic race for Congress in the vain hope of turning the thinking around in Washington and to upgrade the nation's sorry health care system. The pundits had written off Doc's candidacy from the day of his announcement, terming the race unwinnable for any challenger. The incumbent shared that view and it apparently went to his head.

Oops. Large egos tend to crowd out real thinking. So not everyone was surprised when it was intimated in a local alternative weekly that the Congressman was enjoying an intimate dalliance with one of his campaign aides. Then the story jumped to the headlines of the mainstream media. This happened when the husband of the aide found the dalliers twixt the sheets at a motel in another county. He registered his displeasure by emptying both barrels of a twelve-gauge...at the television on which they had been watching a dirty movie. No one was hurt, but the incumbent took the cue. He promptly and appropriately withdraw his candidacy. He still won 20% of the vote. Linda Lovelace fans, perhaps.

So Doc went to Washington, and though he didn't make sea changes, he did raise high the banner of awareness about the nation's worsening health crisis. He also remembered who had sent him to represent them, earning high marks during his first term because he paid serious attention to the needs of his constituents. So happy were the locals with his service that Doc became something of a biennial favorite in the voting booth. He was consistently in the eightieth percentile in public support, and for the second decade of his service he drew only titular opposition. But he never let it go to his head.

Francie couldn't imagine what Doc might need help about, or why they should meet out of the public eye, as he had apparently requested. Their mutual friend had told Doc that one of Francie's favorite walks was from Monastery Beach over to the mouth of the Carmel River, so they set up a meeting for the next morning on a bench above the beaten path with a gorgeous view of Point Lobos – when the fog lifted, if it lifted – and very few fellow travelers.

Francie was three minutes early as usual and Doc was precisely on time. She liked that. Politicians usually had egos the size of Delaware, and doctors were notorious about keeping people waiting. This man held both titles but didn't suffer from either condition. The Congressman was an inch or two over six feet and slightly stooped, probably from greeting and treating so many smaller people. Thin but not gaunt, with an angular face and a full head of greyish hair, cut shorter than long. He looked healthier than his sixty-eight years by maybe a decade, but not this morning because worry and/or a lack of sleep had taken a toll.

They sat down on the bench. He looked around. "Good spot," he said.

"We shouldn't be over-heard," she said, responding to his observation.

His eyes narrowed slightly as he peered at her briefly. She could see that he had made a quick and affirmative judgement about her, no doubt atop what he had heard about her from their friend.

"What can I do for you?" she asked, respecting his time.

"Right to the point," he said. "I like that. Thank you.

She gave him a brief nod.

"You probably know that while I have been in Congress, I have kept my office open. I have a young doctor and my old nurse. I shouldn't put it that way; she's not so old but I mean that she's been with me for years. They've been holding down the fort. I don't see patients anymore, except maybe a few who really need me, but I consult with Jeremy – Jeremy Barrett, he's the doctor, very bright young man – Harvard and then Yale Medical School – and I consult with him when he needs me."

Doc sighed and then continued, "And Eileen Adler is the nurse. A real workhorse, and a favorite with the patients. She is the epitome of the attentive health care worker who knows everyone who walks in the door."

"And the problem?"

"The problem is that someone is stealing drugs from the office."

"As in?"

"Vicodin and OxyContin."

"Why haven't you called in the police? They're pretty good about finding out who's doing that sort of thing."

Doc was quiet. Francie suddenly knew why. She gave him a moment to explain, but when he didn't, she did.

"Oh," she said. "You know who it is."

He looked her hard in the eyes. "I was told you were sharp. I didn't realize..."

"It was one of two things," Francie said to him patiently. "Either you were worried about the political repercussions, but that didn't seem like you, or it was someone you didn't want to confront."

He looked in her face, nodding his grey head slowly, appreciative of her mind. "Yes, it's Eileen."

"Ouch," Francie said, sharing his pain that it was his long-time, once-trusted nurse who was pilfering the drugs. "How sure are you?"

"I'm sure," he told her, taking a deep breath and letting it out again. "But I don't have any proof. I can't force it without proof. That's why I asked to see you. You have a reputation for discretion."

Francie didn't need to tell him that discretion was not a likely outcome. "But she had to know that at some point the fact that drugs were missing would be noticed." Francie knew this from her reporter days, "You must have regular inventories of Schedule I drugs."

"Of course, it's required by law." He stopped there.

"Ahhh," Francie said, realizing the situation. "She's the person who does the inventory."

Doc nodded his head again. It had taken him a while to come to grips with the problem and now the whole story had come out in a matter of minutes.

"Have you spoken to her about this at all, even to mention that you thought some drugs might be missing? Or to Dr. Barrett?"

He shook his head. "No, I knew it was Eileen, but I didn't know what to say to her."

"So you don't know what she is stealing the drugs for?" she asked.

He looked at her somewhat surprised.

Francie continued, "She's not using the stuff herself. You would have noticed that. So is she selling it or giving it to someone." She saw a light go on in his head and then immediately the wheels were turning, albeit it in the wrong direction. "No," she insisted to him firmly, "This is not something you can handle yourself."

His face showed surprise that she had read him, and the surprise gave way to the deeper, unhappy second thoughts that he'd ever opened up this Pandora's Box. But he was also a bright man, and not a coward, and he knew that regret would not close the case.

She laid it on the line for him. "Surely you've seen enough of this problem, Doc, to know that reason doesn't work. Especially with someone you've trusted all these years. Whoever she's stealing the drugs for is more important to her than you, than your practice, than your position in Congress. That's pretty ruthless. That's not your arena, even though you've been in Washington all this time." It was a joke. It wasn't funny.

The realization of her truth drained the energy out of him, but then he realized that she was in fact lifting the responsibility for dealing with the situation off of his shoulders. A range of emotions was expressed in his features as he looked at her. She let him look. She didn't want him to have any more doubts, not any more than were necessary.

Finally, he relented against his better wishes and adjusted himself to the new reality. "What's next? How do you work? Do I give you a retainer?"

That was encouraging, not about getting the money, but it showed that he had turned responsibility of the matter over to her. Francie replied, "I won't tell you how I work or what's next. I think it's better that you have complete deniability about what happens."

Alarm showed on his face. She explained, "You can be assured that I will act in your best interests, for your constituents and your patients, but it's not likely that this will turn out well for your nurse. I think the best thing would be for me to wait until you are back in Washington. When will that be?"

"We're in recess for the rest of the month. I'll be working in the district until then. I've got a full schedule of constituent meetings and public events. And a fundraiser or two."

"Does she have access to her own personnel file?"

"No," he said, smiling. "I always trusted her, but that wouldn't have been correct."

"I'd like to get a look at it."

The Doc chuckled for the first time since he'd sat down. "I had a feeling you might. I have it in the car," he said, and nodded in the direction of the parking area.

"Good for you," she told him, not in the least patronizing. This was going to be hard for him, but not as bad as it might have been if he had tried to deal with it himself. "And as far as the costs, I don't know how this will play out, but I expect that ten thousand will cover everything. If it gets more complicated, I'll let you know."

He raised his eyebrows at the price. "I didn't realize it would be that much," he told her, but his tone was clear that he wasn't negotiating, just confirming verbally what his eyebrows had indicated.

"I'd like a $2,500 retainer to start, please," Francie said when she saw that he wasn't changing his mind. And she added, "I can assure you that when this is all over, you'll be quite satisfied with the amount you will pay."

He smiled at her. "I know that. My checkbook is also in the car."

They got up from the bench and walked across the top of the hill. The meadow on their right and Carmel Bay on their left were so distant in their natural tranquility from the new problem Francie had to face. In two minutes they arrived at the end of a path which was where the road dead-ended and hikers parked their cars. His car was an older BMW with a faded bumpersticker that read "Doc = Rx". Francie recognized it from a campaign that went back several cycles. He had indeed been a prescription, of sorts. He had gotten some important health care legislation through the storied halls of Congress that wouldn't have become law if he hadn't been there. Not everything that the country needed – he was fighting enormously entrenched and well-financed interests – but it was an important step forward.

He took a file folder from a beaten-up leather briefcase in the trunk, checked to make sure it was the right one and handed it to her. Then he pulled out a checkbook and wrote out the retainer. She watched his face as he did so. Unlike some of her clients who had shown doubt in their eyes as they took this first step, Doc knew what he was doing. So did Francie, but that was for him to find out when the job was done.

As she walked back across the meadow to her own car parked by the Bay School, she felt an unpleasant tingling at the base of her spine. No, she knew, this wasn't going to be an open-and-shut case – actually, they never were – but this one smelled of a hidden danger. Drug cases were never easy, mainly because they often took place down the pharmaceutical rabbit hole. That's what drugs did to people, when they took too many of them. Drugs not only killed pain, physical and emotional, but they distorted reality. And with reality went reason and morality. Francie knew that she would have to be particularly alert, to always be vigilant and not to be sure of anything she thought she knew.

She arrived at this conclusion and her car at the same time as a cold breeze blew over the water. She knew it was a sign. She didn't know of what.

*   *   *   *   *

Francie LeVillard knew from her years as a television news reporter and now as a consulting detective that the first place to start in a case when you knew the crime and the criminal was to figure out the motive. Francie needed to know why Nurse Adler was stealing the Vicodin and Oxycontin. Her instincts told her that this was personal, and she went online to see if she could find the evidence to provide at least the preliminary confirmation of her feelings, or maybe a new direction in which to look. Because of prior cooperation with local law enforcement on a number of cases that ranged across the Monterey Peninsula – and some well beyond – Francie had earned certain discreet privileges that were unofficial and based entirely on personal relationships.

For instance, there was Mike Olsen, who was attached to the FBI office in San Jose but worked out of his home near Salinas. He and Francie had worked together on several cases during which they had developed mutual high regard. In one of her investigations, Francie had turned up evidence of a terrorist ring trying to smuggle a nuclear trigger into the United States. In another she had discovered that a couple of Mexican cartel hit men were using phony INS identification to operate in the southwest. They had made the mistake of coming to Monterey.

So it was that when Francie, infrequently, asked Olsen if she could check out some leads that normally weren't accessible to private investigators, he gave her the appropriate computer access codes. To cover him and protect herself, she had set up her computer (with the invaluable help of her "spook" friend Ariane Chevasse) to mask her entry to all of the places where she might be looking. If anyone happened upon her trail, which was highly unlikely to begin with, they would find that it led to a public access computer in a library in Fullerton.

Before she looked behind the secrets curtain, however, Francie googled the nurse's name and came up with...almost nothing. Less than a handful of newspaper items that mentioned her as one of Doc Hardwicke's medical support staff while he was in Our Nation's Capitol, and one short bit from way back about her losing her husband in a car wreck. According to that article, Eileen Adler was driving, wearing a seatbelt, and their infant son was in a baby seat in the back. They both came through the accident unscathed, but the husband/father, who had not been wearing a belt, had gone through the windshield.

It didn't have to mean anything, but a little light went off in the back of Francie's suspicions-tuned brain. The accident had occurred twenty-four years earlier, which would make the son today of prime drug age. There was nothing else about the accident in the news archives. It was an old story and most of the law enforcement types working at the time would have retired, but that didn't mean they would have lost their memory, nor their instincts.

Next Francie googled the son. As an infant, Garry had his father's last name, Debb, and nothing turned up, but then on a hunch she checked "Garry Adler," and bang-zoom, there were a handful of stories about arrests; three traffic stops, including driving without a license and failure to stop, and – surprise, surprise – two drug busts. Both were for small amounts of heroin.

Francie knew that the newspapers showed Adler's name only because he was over eighteen at the time of those arrests. If he'd been arrested earlier, the papers would have only described him as a nameless juvenile. She could check that later, but she already knew that she would find that he had had prior run-ins with the law. She shifted her attention back to the mother, and plying through county records she discovered that the widow had taken sole title to their house in Carmel Valley after the husband was killed. That was to be expected. Francie also read that she had paid off the balance of the mortgage, probably with insurance money. Not unusual, of course, but again that little light went on.

More searching, and then she found..."Bingo." Adler's husband had had a half-million dollar policy on his life, with a double indemnity payoff. That was a bit unusual, both the high amount and the two-fer, especially for a working couple. And sweet, Francie thought, for the two remaining Adlers. She wondered if she would turn up any evidence of marital difficulties before the, um, accident.

As pleased as she was with what she had managed to learn in just forty-five minutes online, Francie was aware of that feeling again; that this was more perilous than it had at first appeared. She sat back and took a deep breath. The last time she had felt that tingling in her lowest chakra, she had been thinking that a sweet little old lady she was investigating couldn't possibly be a murderer times four.

Suddenly the woman had sprung at her with a meat cleaver, trying to make her number five. Francie had ended the killer granny's career by firing her Beretta .25 Bobcat at the woman, but it had taken three shots – all good hits – to stop her. It was after that that she had moved up to a .357 magnum S&W with much more heft. The cleaver had grazed Francie's hip.

Francie left her office and walked into the kitchen to brew a cup of tea. Thinking back to her talk with the Doc, she realized that he, too, had known that this wasn't a simple case of theft. She was clear now that she would need to find out all she could about both this woman and her son before she took to the stage. And it would have to be she herself who would set the scene.

A steaming mug in her hand, she returned to her desk. Her next look was at the nurse's bank records. What she discovered was that even after paying off the house, she still had four hundred thousand dollars, which she had placed in three different banks in three states. That seemed fairly conclusive that stealing the drugs was not about avarice. Not with the stolen drugs being worth under $5,000, according to Doc Hardwicke.

Intuitively Francie had known the woman wasn't stealing because she couldn't afford to give her son the money to buy the drugs. Which still left that huge motive gap. Also disturbing was that the nurse had to know that eventually the pilfered drugs would be missed. It could be that there was a time factor – some kind of urgent need for the drugs – but it didn't feel like that. There had to be an explanation; juries don't convict without a motive. From past investigations, Francie knew that when the motive wasn't immediately clear, she needed to tread very carefully.

She had several options for how to proceed, and she also wasn't in a hurry for a confrontation. With Doc not heading back to Washington right away, she had the time to be that very careful. She decided to put her ear to the ground, as they say, and listen to the rumblings. There was a fellow she knew on The Peninsula who was well-connected in ways the police weren't; though they certainly wished they could be. This was a guy who was tied into the Sicilian community where the community telegraph knew just about everything about everyone, for better or worse.

Francie gave a ring at his store in Sand City. He was there. Of course, he said, he could see her. She heaved a big sigh. This was a delicate move generally. When you ask for information, you risk giving some away. This man heard a lot, and "paid" for it in kind. She didn't want her investigation to become public, not yet.

Angelo Crespino was the large and loud owner of Big A's Rental in Sand City. Their motto was "You Wanna, We Gotta" and it did very well for him. Plus, he had family working for him at minimum wage, when they were on the books, and they did everything from filling propane tanks to pouring champagne at parties. His gorgeous daughter handled outside sales and his less gorgeous but fierce wife kept the books.

It wasn't that Angelo was so large – he says five-ten and 250 pounds though he was a little high on the first and a bunch low on the second – but he had natural and powerful presence. His laughter could fill a room. More to the point, he did a lot of favors for people. No one who knew him ever went hungry, and others had borrowed money that they still owed years later. Sometimes they did favors for Angelo.

He wasn't a godfather, by any stretch of the imagination. He didn't have people killed, though when someone needed it, they might be brought out behind the proverbial woodshed for a, um, talking to. Nothing that would upset the police. In fact, they appreciated Angelo's role in the community. He maintained a degree of order that law enforcement wouldn't have been able to match if they had tried, and they were glad they didn't have to. He would often provide them with information when a situation required official intervention, especially if those involved were outside of the Italian and Sicilian communities.

Francie spent some time in the kitchen making pans and dishes messy and then headed to Sand City

*   *   *   *   *

Angelo and Francie were on the same side, especially after she had helped Sal Domenico, one of the more successful businessman in the area, pull his daughter out from under the influence of some nefarious con artists. Sal's imprimatur meant a lot, so when Francie had gone to Angelo for "advice" a number of cases back, he was interested to meet the "white girl detective" who had scored so high with a higher-up in his circle. And ever the businessman, he wanted to make sure that if she needed to rent anything, she would rent from Big A's Rental.

By the time she dropped by on the Doc Hardwicke case, Crespino considered Francie a confidant. She would always bring him something when she came to pick his brain, usually a freshly-made something that he could smell when she walked through the door. The way to a man's heart, they say, is down the gullet. On this occasion she brought him a tub of chopped chicken liver. It was from an abridged version of a recipe she'd learned in New York that included bacon.

"Whassat?" he demanded, staring at the container she was carrying with a fresh baguette she'd picked up on the way at La Bicyclette in Carmel. Francie put the container on the counter and waved the baguette in front of his face. "It's bread," she told him. "What did you think it was?"

"I know that part," he said garrulously, "but what's that?"

"Close your eyes," she ordered. This was not a new routine so he complied. She opened the lid and raised the container to a few inches below his nose. He sniffed noisily, opened his eyes, peered at the chopped liver, and asked in his best, if uneducated, Brooklynese, "Chopt livah?"

"That's right, Angelo. I thought you deserved a treat." She broke off a piece of the bread and used it as a scoop to deliver the treat to its destination. He took it from her, examined it, sniffed it again, and then put a large bite in his mouth. He chewed tentatively at first, and then, with approvingly "mmm" sounds as he masticated more enthusiastically.

"Oh, my, that is good," he said, as he tore off another piece of bread and started the process again. This time he chewed more slowly, savoring the textures and the flavors. When he was done, he turned his head sideways, granted her a broad smile from both his mouth and the facing eye. "Ya know, Francie, you cook like this, you don't even have to be good-looking, and you are that, too. I don't understand how you ain't married."

"Oh, Angelo, you say the nicest things...I think. But the fact is that the guy would have to be so wonderful, I wouldn't come to town any more and then what would you do?"

"Starve!" Angelo answered. He fed himself again. When he was done, oohing and aahing his way through his third taste, he said, "So you want something big, I guess, huh?"

She lowered her voice. "Not so big, Angelo. Maybe nothing at all. I don't know. I was wondering if you knew a guy?"

"Knew a guy? Here on The Peninsula?"

She nodded.

"Come on, I know everybody. What's his name?"

She leaned forward slightly and told him, "I know you are the soul of discretion, but this is particularly important. If he heard that I was asking, there could be problems, you know?"

"Trust me, Francie," he said, showing a hurt expression.

"Don't feed me that hang-dog stuff, Angelo. I don't know what I'm dealing with yet, and that's why I'm talking to you. A really good guy is maybe in the sights of this bad guy, and I wouldn't want anything to happen to him."

"Okay, I know, all right. So who is it?"

"Garry Alder," she told him quietly.

Crespino tilted his head back, raising his eyebrows as he looked down his face at her. "*Pericoloso*," he said in a tone she hadn't heard often from him. "Dangerous. Maybe *matto*, crazy. He is not someone you want to be around, if you listen to me.

Francie was taken by the sharpness in his voice. "That's what I wanted to know, Angelo. I'll be careful. I thought maybe that was the case. What is he into? Drugs?"

Angelo looked around to make sure that no one was in earshot. "I don't think he sells, but maybe he uses, you know? Heroin, I think. Maybe methamphetamines, too."

She had another question, one that she knew would tread on his own cultural sensitivities, even though the person in question wasn't Mediterranean. She lowered her voice further. "Anything on Eileen Adler?"

He stared at her for a long time, or maybe it was just a few seconds, but it was tangible. "What?" she asked him.

"You don't want to get mixed up with her. She is *maligna*," he said. "You know that word?"

"Malignant, I'd guess."

"Yes, malignant. She is evil."

"Whew, I've really nailed it with you today, Angelo, haven't I?"

"I'm telling you they are not good to be with, those two. I look out for you, Francie. You listen to me."

"I appreciate that, Angelo, I really do, and I will be careful," she promised him. "But tell me, what do you know about her that she is evil. I thought she was a nurse."

Angelo looked around again. "I can't say for sure, you

know. It was a long time ago..."

"But...?"

"I think maybe she murdered her husband."

"That's not nice," she said, "but lots of wives do that. Okay, maybe not lots, but it sounds special to you. Did she do it for the money?"

Angelo shook his head, "That's not what I heard. Not the money, but she got a lot of it. It was how she did it."

"How did she do it?"

He tiled his head back again and said, "She crashed their car into a tree. She had her baby in the back seat and she drove into a tree on his side of the car."

"Ick," Francie said. "That is ugly. Sick."

"Maligna," Angelo repeated.

"But why?"

Angelo shook his head, "I don't know." He leaned forward again. "But I don't think it's very, you know" – he looked down at the chopped liver – "kosher, between her and the son," he said.

Her eyes widened. "You mean...?"

Angelo cringed, "I don't know about that, you know, but you don't have to do that for it to be weird, right?"

"Right," she agreed and thought, stealing drugs from your boss-the-doctor for no apparent reason was weird enough, but this, too?

*　　　*　　　*　　　*　　　*

Since she was sort of in the neighborhood, Francie drove up to the airport to chat up her friend, Marla Melas. Marla was the admin assist, as she referred to herself, in the security department. Actually she was far more important than that. She had worked under four security chiefs during the past ten years, and had showed each of them the ropes. None was fired. Each left with a great record for a larger airport, moves made possible by Marla. Francie asked her how her proteges were all doing, and Marla winced as she told her friend that they had all seemed to stall in their subsequent careers. Francie was not surprised.

Francie's was not a security question, nor did it have anything to do with the wonderful home airport. Her question was how to properly rattle the cages at LuxAir to get her miles restored. Marla wasn't at all connected to such issues, but over her ten years, she'd made a lot of contacts with the airlines, both locally and at their regional and national offices.

"Oh, darlin'," she said in her ex-pat Texas drawl when Francie had explained her situation, "you are one of ten million victims of these armadillo brains."

"Do I get a prize for that?"

"Just frustration," Marla said with a grimace. The woman used her face for more expressions than Frank Gorshin but it was never as though she was on stage. Rather, she spoke with all her features, and it was artful.

"Know anyone I can yell at?"

Marla's whole face narrowed to a point, which was quite something since normally – normal for her – Marla had a lovely broad expanse that tied the tongue of every healthy male who saw it. Her big black hair complemented the attraction. Men who had no real business with her came through the office regularly just to look, smile, and dream. Marla loved it and she sent them off with a delicious smile of no promise. She came out of her thinking posture and pulled her keyboard closer.

"It may just be..." she said as she tickled the ivories and then stared at the screen. "No, darn it. She's not there any more." More clacking, more staring. "Ahso," she said.

"Ahso?" Francie asked. "That doesn't sound very Dallas."

"Hon, I am a cosmopolitan American. I must be able to speak with everyone. Surely you can appreciate that?"

"Oh, yes, Marla, I'm appreciating you more than I ever knew was possible."

"That's better," Marla said, and they both laughed. She poked a bunch of numbers on the phone and listened, while Francie watched her face put on a show. She heard someone answer at the other end.

"Rachel, honey, Marla M at M-R-Y, how y'all?"

She listened and then said, "Oh, girl, I am so pleased for you. Having your Jimmy-Bob back must be downright wonderful? Is he on probation or is he done?"

More listening, more facing. "Well, I suppose you had to expect that, after what he said to the judge....Uh-huh...Uh-huh...Uh-huh...Well, it's good you got all of the hooch out of the house. Let's hope for the best...Uh-huh, well let me tell you why I rang, aside to check up on my best pal in Cleveland...you, too...I've got a friend who's been having trouble getting through the blockheads in your customer service...Yeah, I know everyone does, but she's a special lady, and I was wondering if there was someone you know she could call – maybe in this country – who could fix the screw-up, if you know what I mean."

Marla had a pen at the ready and in a moment she was writing.

"That's great, girl, I am so your best-est friend in Monterey... Right, all of California. And ditto you for Ohio...uh-huh...uh-huh...Sure will. Kisses." And with that she hung up on the phone. She handed the paper with a name and phone number on it to Francie. "I wish I could tell you I was optimistic, hon, but Rachel wasn't, so I can only tell you good luck."

"Oh, Marla, honey, you are my best-est friend in all of the airlines everywhere on the planet," Francie gushed. They laughed together and Francie left her to her real work.

As she drove back down the coast to her home by Yankee Point – at the south end of the Carmel Highlands, if you need a point of reference – she marveled at the scope of her life. From Angelo Crespino to Marla Melas, they didn't define the range of the species by any means, but they certainly made her life richer. She supposed one could find people like them anywhere, or maybe not, and maybe that's why they were on the Monterey Peninsula. They were certainly two reasons why Francie was there.

She arrived at her humble 2,500-square foot ranch house twenty-five yards back from a twenty-five foot drop to the rocky coastline that met with the Pacific Ocean. Her house, which size-wise was the runt of the local domicile litter, was her sanctuary. She backed into the driveway, as she always did – Boy Scouts weren't the only ones who thought it was important to Be Prepared – and walked up to the front door. She raised a three-inch square metal flap and pressed her left thumb against the surface underneath. There was a click and she pushed the door open.

With the kind of work she did, she had plenty of grateful clients, but also some people who were not happy with the "success" that filtered down to them. Most of them had the sense to stay out of her way, but it wouldn't have been sensible on her part not to take precautions. She had some very smart security folks her friend Ariane knew who put together a system that made her feel comfortable. No panic room, but she didn't want to go overboard, especially not when most of the west wall of the house was glass. Plus Francie was a very good shot.

The main part of the house was one large room, with the kitchen to the east, looking up toward the coastal range that climbed up on the other side of the Pacific Coast Highway. It was a good-sized kitchen for someone who lived alone, with a large prep island, Vulcan's home version of a professional stove, and two sinks. She played a lot in that kitchen, for which Angelo and other friends were grateful. There was a walk-through area and then the living and dining area. On the south side of the house were her bedroom suite and a second bedroom that she used as an office. On the north side was another bedroom suite for the infrequent guests that she allowed to share her space, along with a pantry, more closet space, and the entrance to the garage.

She loved her house, for it was decorated to her taste with her things, from the art on the walls to the linens on her bed, and the dishes and flatware. Every time she came home, even if she'd just been to town on errands, she experienced a special feeling of pleasure that she was there, in her sanctuary. Oh, she also had a deck on the west side, along the full length of the house, with a hot tub that was a particularly valued spot for her, especially as the house was situated on the fog-renowned Central Coast. She wouldn't tell how many hours she spent in the tub. You might think she didn't get any work done.

She turned on a flame under the kettle so she might have some tea and went to her office to call the person Marla had dug up for her. The kettle would be whistling in four or five minutes, and she figured either it was the right person and he could handle it in a trice, or she would know in even less time that he wasn't.

Door number two, Monty.

"Hello, I'm calling for Reggie Duquesne."

"I'm sorry, Mr. Duquesne is not available at this time."

"When might he be available?"

There was silence at the other end of the line.

"Hello?" Francie asked, to check if there was still someone there.

"Um, well, we don't know."

"You don't know? Isn't he the vice president in charge of customer service?"

More silence. "He, uh...I don't know."

"Not to be rude, but is there a grown-up there?"

Suddenly she heard muffled crying coming through the phone. "I'm sorry," Francie said, "I didn't mean to hurt your feelings. This has been a very strange conversation. I thought I was calling an executive at a major airlines."

There were sounds of sniffling and then, "No, that's right, you did, only..." and there was more crying.

Francie took the phone away from her head and looked at it in a stage gesture she used when what she was hearing something from it that didn't make sense. It was a response that was required with increasing frequency. She returned the phone to her ear. There was some more sniffling, but she thought it sounded like the person was trying to pull herself together. "Should I call back another time?"

"No," the woman said, "It wouldn't do any good."

"Should I ask why?"

"Because Mr. Duquesne is gone," she said with some vehemence.

"Gone? Did he die?" Francie asked, grasping for straws.

"No, I wish he did." No sniffle, but a gasp. "I shouldn't have said that."

"What should you have said?" Francie coaxed.

"He left. He left for Ecuador on our 1016 out of Miami. He was with Sandi Plitnick. She was my best friend."

"Ah, and you don't expect him back?"

"He left his wife and five children for that floozy." More sniffling.

"Your best friend is a floozy?" She wished she had been recording this.

"I didn't know that but she was. He was such a nice man, too. I don't know what happened."

"Uh-huh," Francie said, and decided it was time to cut her losses. "I think my kettle is getting ready to whistle," she told her, for whatever the truth was worth..

"What?"

She'd finally gotten her attention. "Not to worry, ma'am," Francie said in a comforting tone. "I'm sure it will all work out."

"You really think so?" the woman asked.

Francie could almost see her face brightening. "Oh, sure. Why don't you go to the ladies room and fix your face. Give yourself a big smile in the mirror, and you'll see that things will get better."

"Well thanks, I will."

The kettle began to whistle. Francie hung up the phone and chuckled her way to the kitchen.

*   *   *   *   *

There are many spiritual traditions, particularly in the black arts, where the practitioner wants to hold a piece from the subject of a rite in her hand – maybe a lock of hair or a piece of their clothing – or at least to behold that person, up close and personal, for even a moment, to feel them. Something that brings their energy to the party, so to speak. Francie wasn't trying to get a piece of these people, at least not yet. But she did want to get a better personal feel for whom she was dealing with, so she drove out to Carmel Valley to get a look at their house.

Their house was actually two houses; one a smaller, carbon copy of the other. The main house was probably 1400 square feet and the small unit was probably half that size. The main house sat closer to the road while the smaller unit was in a right rear corner of the lot. They were both simple, single story buildings with pale green aluminum siding. It looked like the contractor had gotten a deal on materials and built the contractee a house and an in-law unit at the same time.

Before Francie had driven out, she had checked the area for similar addresses. Indeed, their property was on Calabasas Drive and not too far away was Calabasas Court. She had also pulled out one of her favorite props. It was a pad that she'd had printed up with the name and logo of a non-existent real estate company. On the top sheet she had written "Rental" then beneath it the correct street number of the house, and "Calabasas Court." Francie tore off the page, as she would have gotten it from a realtor, and set off for a look-see.

Her ride out to the Valley had been delayed until Doc Hardwicke had left Monterey for his day job, which was as a member of Congress. Francie had told him she didn't want to step onto the stage, as it were, with him in town. He had departed for Washington after the end of the summer break.

Francie drove out to the address and got out of her car, clutching the piece of paper as she walked up to the main house. It being a Tuesday morning at 10:30, she expected the homeowner – and drug theft suspect – Eileen Adler to be on the job at Doc's office. Francie didn't just presume; she had called the Doc to confirm Adler's schedule. Also, there was no car in the drive-way. Of course it was possible that the son was home – she was guessing in the rear unit – and it was for him that she had brought the piece of paper.

She knocked on the front door. Waited. Knocked again. Then she did what any potential renter would do; she walked around the house looking through the windows. The walking she could do, but not the looking. The blinds were lowered on all of the windows, and there were drapes closed behind the blinds, even in the back of the house. She had circled the house and then stopped, pondered, and walked toward the smaller house. From what she could see as she approached, the blinds and drapes were the same, and similarly positioned.

When she was about ten feet away, the front door suddenly opened wide and a young man appeared, standing on the door sill. He was barefoot, wearing worn jeans, and no shirt. His skin was white and looked more so because he had Goth tattoos on his arms, chest and neck. She recognized him, however, from his booking photo in the news accounts; he was Garry Adler.

"Oh,"she said, pretending surprise. "Hi, I'm here about the rental."

He stood still, looking her over in a way that made her want to take a shower. "Are you the owner?" she asked brightly. She approached gingerly. "My real estate agent said this property was for rent." She held up the piece of paper and gave him her best confused expression.

He didn't take the paper but he looked at it. "Ain't for rent," he said.

"Oh, but it says..."

"You got the wrong address. This is Calabasas Drive. That says Court."

She might have given him credit for noticing, and even asked directions to the other location, but there wasn't the opportunity. He stepped back and shut the door firmly.

"Oh," she said again, for effect to no one at all. She stood for a moment, then turned and walked back to her car, as any innocent would. In case he was watching, she took out a map and looked at it as if she were searching for the correct address. Then she drove off.

She reflected on what she had experienced about the house. It wasn't overtly intimidating like the house above the Bates Motel, but with all the windows covered, there was a cloistered feeling about the place. As regards the young man, Francie thought Angelo's description – dangerous and crazy – were pretty much on the money. She wouldn't see him again without a bullet in the chamber of her gun.

Next on her agenda was to see the nurse herself, and what better venue than the Doc's office. As might be expected, his brief time back in the district meant that he didn't see many patients, and Francie had set it up with him that her appearance at his office didn't require that he be there. He would have her come to his office to pick up a prescription for Fluocinolone (for eczema) but he needed her to first fill out an inpatient form at his office.

Francie knew she was taking a risk that the son would call his mother to mention her visit, but she didn't think that she had made such an impression on him that he needed to phone her rather than waiting until she had come home to tell her, if ever. Still, she took off the blue-checked shirt she'd worn to Calabasas Drive and put on an ochre vest over her tee shirt. She also lost the sunglasses that the son had seen her wearing. Walking into the Doc's waiting room, she used her energy and posture to make herself seem unimportant.

Nurse Adler handed her a clipboard with a three-page patient history form and a pen. Francie thanked her quietly and went across the room to fill it out. And to check her out. She already knew that she was 46 from scanning her records. With her undyed hair which she wore pulled back tightly into a bun, she looked older, and cold. The white uniform didn't help; she needed some color but she wore no make-up. She never stood up, but Francie's impression was that she wasn't a large woman, maybe a couple of inches shorter than her son who was probably five-ten.

In the time it took Francie to carefully fill out the forms, she watched the nurse interact with the medical assistant and two patients, and handle a couple of calls. She was all business, and somewhere between tired and, sigh, patient. There was also a brief interchange with Doctor Barrett who came out from the back. Francie wouldn't say he seemed intimidated talking to the nurse, but it certainly wasn't the high point of his day. Francie noted, however, that he gave herself a pleasant smile before he disappeared back into the examination area.

Francie didn't want to appear to be an idiot with the paperwork – she preferred to give no impression at all – so she didn't dawdle beyond reason. When she returned the clipboard to Nurse Adler, she kept her eyes down, and waited for her to go through it to clear her.

"Looks okay," she said. "Here's your prescription," she added, handing her the slip. Then Francie noticed that the woman narrowed her gaze at her, as though she recognized Francie, but she didn't say anything. She managed a half-smile. Francie returned it and left.

On her way home, Francie sorted through her observations and feelings about the woman. She not only scanned what she had seen and heard and felt, but she revisited the recollections from the perspective of how she might have appeared if Francie hadn't known anything about her. While maligna didn't rise to the top of the list of descriptions, Francie also wouldn't have sat next to her on a bus. From what she had read and seen, Francie would have been surprised to discover that the Doc and Angelo were wrong about the woman.

*   *   *   *   *

"*Allo, fille amie,*" Francie said when Ariane Chevasse answered the phone.

"I know it is you," she said in her delicious French accent which she had made no effort to shed over her decades of living in the United States. "But what, pray tell, is '*fille amie*'?"

"Glad you asked, Ariane. You know how they use the expression 'girlfriend' here all the time?"

"*Oui, bien sûr, c'est absurde.*"

"I was just trying out the French version. *Fille amie*...girl friend."

"Ah, and I am of the great hope that you perhaps had another reason to call, yes?"

"But of course...," Francie replied in her own French accent.

They both laughed.

"Here's the deal," she said. "I need you to put some electronic gear in a doctor's office for me. Nothing fancy. Maybe a no-light camera and a couple of ears."

"*Mais, c'est possible, certainement,* but will this doctor know?"

"Actually, yes, and that's the point."

"Oh, so you want to force something, is that it?"

"You are so smart, Ariane, no wonder we are friends."

"Both ways, girlfriend," she said, and they laughed again. Then Francie explained what she wanted Ariane to do.

*   *   *   *   *

Francie called Doc Hardwicke to let him know what she was doing and to have him fax a letter of authorization to Ariane, which she could show to Doctor Barrett and Nurse Adler, to allow her to install security devices in the medical offices. Ariane went in to see them on Friday and informed them that she would do the work on Saturday afternoon. Their operation would not be disrupted because the office closed at noon. She was given a set of keys.

Francie's presumption was that Nurse Adler or her son would want to go in Friday night. It should be, she told herself, a piece of cake to make a bust. She got it partly right.

Ariane and Francie went in right after close of business on Friday. They put in the two audio bugs, one near the front door and one in the examining room where the drugs were kept. That was where Ariane also placed the camera. It was a remarkably simple operation that took only ten minutes, because the devices didn't need to be hidden, and Francie expected to need them only for the next twelve hours. She got that part right.

Francie had made arrangements with a realtor friend who had a vacant office space across the street where she could park herself with her laptop, with some coffee and sandwiches, to monitor the set stage in the medical office sixty feet away. Monterey being a fairly quiet town, at least after five in the doctor's row area, she didn't imagine that she would have to wait until three in the morning, if the Adlers were going to be making their entry at all. She got that part right, too.

At eleven-thirty, she happened to be looking down Cass Street, facing south, when along came a car, moving slowly. It pulled over to the curb a block away, and after thirty seconds or so, the driver's door opened and Garry Adler emerged. He looked all around and then walked quickly to the front door of the doctor's office. He had a key. He was in immediately. His entrance was corroborated by the sound picked up by the first office bug. Francie waited until she heard him on the second bug and then made her way across the street.

She skirted the man's car to make sure no one was in it; it was empty. She had a copy of the key given to Ariane, but out of curiosity she checked the doorknob and found that it was locked. She didn't know if the guy was covering his back. She suspected that it was auto-locking. She noiselessly let herself in and quickly checked to find that the latch was in fact auto-locking. By the light of a fish tank in the reception area Francie made her way to the examining room.

Garry Adler obviously wasn't worried about being discovered. She could hear him moving about and not far away. She eased down the hallway and through the open door she could see a flashlight working. There were only a couple of small windows high up, but he wouldn't have wanted to put on the room lights.

Francie did, closing her eyes first and then opening them slowly. There was plenty of time. He wasn't a deer, but the lights had the same effect.

"Game's up, Mr. Adler," she said, taking a step into the room.

"Hey, what's this?" He peered at her. There was a flash of recognition on his face. "You're that woman who was looking for that house to rent back a coupla weeks." He was partly confused and increasingly upset.

Suddenly he stood a little taller, and if she had had time to realize it, his expression turned smug. But Francie didn't have time to realize what she was seeing. At that moment she felt the cold steel of the muzzle of a gun under her left ear.

Most people using guns in nefarious fashion are amateurs. They expect a person who has a gun pointed at them to freeze. Francie was never one to fulfill expectations. Plus her years of aikido training had taught her to react spontaneously. She didn't have to think about what was happening. Instantly she pivoted to her right, bringing her right hand down on the arm holding the gun. Her chop was so hard she could hear the snap as she broke the ulna. Out of the corner of her eye, she saw the arm fall and then heard the gun clatter on the linoleum floor.

Francie didn't watch it happen because she was following through with her left hand. Slightly cupped she swung it against the ear of the would-be shooter, shattering the ear drum. The heel of her hand slammed against where the lower jaw connected with the skull and disconnected them. The victim emitted a strangled scream that turned into a deep low moan.

Francie reached down to pick up the gun but was stopped by a nasty voice.

"Hold it," said Garry Adler. He was pointing a small snub-nosed revolver at her, but his attention was on the figure crumpled on the floor moaning.

Francie had had no idea when she swung at the assailant who it was, but after the flurry of motion and seeing her on the floor, she recognized Eileen Adler. She must have come in another car and seen her enter the office, she thought. Or she saw the lights in the examining room come on.

Actually those thoughts came later. What her mind was dealing with at the moment was a dangerous man pointing a gun at her. He was looking at her, and leering, as he raised the weapon and aimed it deliberately at the center of her chest. She thought she saw his trigger finger flexing.

Suddenly there was a shot from behind her. Francie's first realization was that she hadn't been shot. Her second was hearing a yelp from son Adler and seeing blood spurting from the arm holding the gun, above the elbow. His forearm fell. The gun dropped to the floor. Francie turned carefully and saw, standing in the doorway, Ariane Chevasse, holding a very unladylike semi-automatic of the .40 caliber variety, a slight trickle of smoke rising from the muzzle.

"Are you all right?" Ariane asked, her eyes shifting quickly from the son holding his arm to the mother moaning on the floor, and then to Francie.

"I'm fine," Francie said, knowing in very real terms the meaning of understatement. She wanted to know how and why Ariane was there, but the first step was to secure the room. While Ariane held the gun on the young man, Francie went over and pushed him away from his gun on the floor and picked it up. Then she grabbed his mother's gun and stood back.

"Glad to see you," she told Ariane.

"What do you people say? We aim to please," she replied, her gun held as steady as if it were sitting on a tripod.

Francie went over to a phone on the wall and dialed 911. A lot of people do that on Friday nights, everywhere in the country. Monterey County was no exception, but she only had to wait for four rings before she heard "Emergency dispatch." Sometimes the voice is even, maybe bored. Not on weekend nights. It was a mixture of tense and tired.

"This is a code 45. I'm Francie LeVillard, a friend of the force." That alerted the dispatcher that the caller was known to the police and could be trusted. "Two wounded, one gun shot, not life-threatening. Situation stabilized. We need an ambulance and a squad car," she reported and then gave dispatch the location. "I'll be standing out front."

They didn't get a lot of calls like that at emergency dispatch so it took a few seconds for the operator to process what he'd heard, but then he was right on it. He said, "On our way. Do you need to stay on the line?"

"Negative. We're all right here," she told him and hung up the phone. It wasn't thirty seconds later that they could hear the sirens. The Monterey police station was only four blocks away. Francie patted down Eileen Adler and then her son. They had no more weapons. She ordered the man to get down on the floor. Holding his arm, blooding flowing through his fingers, he resisted with a loud moan. She kicked him hard on the side of his right knee, and he went down.

"You okay alone?" she asked Ariane.

"*Oui, bien sûr*," Ariane replied, her voice tinged with excitement and satisfaction. "Please go welcome the police."

*   *   *   *   *

"'Girl friend'," Francie told Ariane, "it somehow seems cheap to me." They were sitting at a table at Bellagio's two hours later, chewing on some gluten-free garlic-anchovy pizza and sucking on Sierra Nevada's. The only other place open at that hour without loud music and raucous crowds was Denny's, and besides, the pizza was quite decent. That they were done with the two women so quickly after a shooting said a lot about the Monterey police. At Francie's urging, the duty commander had called the Chief of Police who vouched for her. They took statements from both women, confirmed that Ariane's gun was her own, that it was properly registered, and that she had a concealed weapons permit. They decided they could wait until later in the morning to call Congressman Hardwicke. Francie and Ariane would be back at ten to provide further details.

The Adlers, mother and son, made a trip up to the hospital. Both were going to take some time to heal, but no one on the white-hats' side seemed the least bothered by the fact. There would be time for the criminals to recover in the medical facility at the county jail pending their trials. Ariane's equipment had done a surprisingly good job of capturing both the picture and sound from the moment Garry Adler had entered the examination room. He had gone right to the medicine cabinet. He had a key to it. Both perps had guns but no carry permits, and they had pointed them at Francie in a way that anyone – like twelve people in a jury box looking at the tape – would have to think they meant to kill her.

"How was it that you were monitoring your bugs?" Francie asked Ariane as she picked up a slice of pizza.

"It made sense, *non*, what you said about that they would make a last try for drugs tonight when they thought the security would go in tomorrow. And I knew that you, ma chere amie, not hey-girlfriend, would be there for the collar. Only I'm glad they didn't kill you."

"Thanks to you." Francie shook her head, "I could have sworn he was going in alone. I could see pretty well that there was no one in his car."

"She was in another car. She must have expected him to do this. And then she saw you going into the office. Voila."

"I also didn't think he was someone who would have a gun. That seemed out of character for him. He was a nasty punk, but I couldn't place him with a gun."

"I think the times are changing, my woman friend."

Francie chuckled, "They sure are. I need to sharpen my wits, or find another line of work."

Ariane waved the notion away, "Bah, non. You are a fine consulting detective. I think maybe you shouldn't go in without back-up, you know?"

Francie looked at this woman who had probably saved her life. With that look of hatred in Garry Adler's eyes, the man who shouldn't have a gun but did, she knew he would not have held back.

"I think you're right, Ariane." She looked at her with a warm smile. "Would that be you?"

"Ah, no, that is not my work," she said leaving no room for argument.

"That's right," she agreed, "You're a spook. Not so gritty."

"No, no, no, I didn't mean it like that, you know that. I will be with you whenever you need me." Her voice was as poignantly loaded as Francie had ever heard. It resonated with friendship, concern, and commitment.

"Ditto you, girlfriend," Francie managed, after she had cleared her throat.

"I think *fille amie* is better," Ariane said. They clinked their bottles together and drank them down.

Ariane drove Francie back to the empty office from where she had been keeping watch. Francie picked up her computer and other items and returned to the street. Looking over at the doctor's office, where hours earlier there had been an ambulance and three squad cars, lights flashing, and yellow tape everywhere, now everything was dark. The blood on the examining room floor had probably dried already, Francie thought, and wondered at where her mind sometimes took her.

"I will see you tomorrow at the police station at ten," she told Ariane as they walked around the corner to where Francie had left her car.

"*Oui, d'accord*," Ariane replied. "Now we get our beauty sleep, I think."

"Good plan," Francie agreed, and put her things on the passenger seat of her car. She stood next to the driver's door and looked at Ariane for a long moment. She reached for words, but they didn't come. It wasn't that she was tired. It was that there were no words for what she wanted to say. Ariane stepped forward and put her arms around Francie and held her. "Thank you," Francie said, but the words only scratched the surface.

"We are sisters, Francie," she said.

Francie let go of her, and holding back tears, she nodded. She would have said goodnight, but she didn't trust herself to speak.

Ariane smiled, turned, and walked away.

Francie got into her car, and drove home, waiting until she was in her house, all snug in her bed, before she broke into tears.

*   *   *   *   *

Ariane was just getting out of her car when Francie pulled into the parking lot of the Monterey Police Department later that morning. She walked over and gave Francie a big hug, and with her hands holding Francie's upper arms she looked into her friend's face carefully. Then she asked, "*Chere amie*, you got some of your beauty rest, yes?"

"I did, thanks to you, Ariane," Francie told her.

"Ah, we are sisters. I told you that."

She let her go, turned, and as they headed for the main entrance, she slipped her arm through Francie's. Francie tossed a quick glance at her and saw a broad deep smile on her face. Another appeared on her own.

Phil Lestrade entered the reception area on the other side of the glass as they were coming through the front door. Upon seeing them, he reversed his step and came over to open the door for them.

"Good morning, ladies," he said cheerfully.

"Hi, Phil," Francie said. "This is Ariane Chevasse, my close friend and colleague."

"And life saver," he said, shaking her hand in both of his. "I, personally, and everyone who knows Francie, am most grateful to you."

Ariane blushed lightly. "We are sisters," she said softly, as though he might understand.

There was a moment's hesitation, and then he did.

"Come in, come in," Phil said, gesturing down the hallway. "My office, Francie," he added, since she knew where it was. It wasn't a large room for the Chief of Police, but it was comfortable, and less intimidating than those of some officers who are in greater need of feeling in control. The two women sat in chairs in front of his desk as the chief went around and sat in his desk chair. He leaned forward on his desk. "Can I offer you coffee or something?"

They shook their heads.

He nodded. "Well, I'm pleased to say that there have been some developments since you were here last night, or earlier this morning, I should say." His face indicated that they were positive developments. "The DA was up with Adler and his mother at the hospital, and both are singing. The mother admitting everything, the son taking no responsibility."

Ariane and Francie looked at each other, sharing smiles of satisfaction.

"And there's more," the chief said, regaining their attention.

"The accident?" Francie said. She had told Ariane about it over their early morning pizza. "The death of the father."

Lestrade looked at her in half-surprise. He knew her too well to be startled any more. "Yeah, exactly." He rubbed his hands together. "The woman from the DA's office told the kid right up front that he was in for three-strike sentencing for the breaking-'n-entering, attempted murder, and use of a gun, and the kid asked for a deal. The assistant DA said maybe, and the kid told her that his mother had told him she had deliberately crashed the car to kill his father so they could have a better life together. It seems that they were, um, very close." He scrunched his face. "I don't know how close but it seemed kinda over the top to me. Anyway, when the ADA confronted the mother, noting that her son had ratted her out it to avoid three strikes, she jumped on board and said it was all true. She wasn't angry at her son. She was still trying to protect him."

The next glance Ariane and Francie shared didn't include smiling.

Ariane asked, "So does that mean the man gets off leniently?" Her displeasure was clear. "He is very dangerous, unbalanced, you know. He was going to kill Francie, and he was going to enjoy it. I saw that in his face."

Francie reached her hand over and gave her friend's shoulder a gentle squeeze. Then to the chief, "He's a sick puppy, Phil."

The chief nodded his head. "Yes and the DA knows that. Even if they drop the B&E down to a misdemeanor as part of the deal, with what he told the ADA about the murder of his father – talk about sick and the acorn not falling far from the tree and all that – he will probably be charged with conspiracy after the fact, on top of everything else, he won't be coming out at least for twenty years, if ever."

"What about the mother?" Francie asked. "She bears most of the responsibility, it seems."

Lestrade shrugged his shoulders, "With the time she's up for, she may never see him again."

"How do you call that," Ariane asked, "poetry and justice?"

"Poetic justice, indeed," the chief said, nodding his head sagely. "Not a poem, but justice at last."

Ariane and Francie signed their statements and soon left the police station. Francie invited her to have some brunch, but Ariane took a rain check. "I feel like a nap," she said. "After the completion, you know?"

Francie knew.

*   *   *   *   *

"I guess I'll need a new head nurse," said Congressman Doc Hardwicke from Washington.

"Yeah, Doc, sorry to put you to the trouble," Francie replied.

"I'm so glad it's over."

Even three thousand miles away, Francie could hear the relief in Doc's voice. "I think people who have that kind of condition or whatever it might be called – bad character – give off vibrations that make life difficult for everyone around them. I suppose the people who came to your office for treatment didn't really notice, because most of them weren't feeling so hot in the first place."

"You did very well, Francie, and I am most grateful."

"You'll need some bismuth when you get my bill."

Her client laughed. "Whatever it is, it will be worth it." Then he added, "And by the way, I don't know if you heard from the district attorney that Eileen also admitted to fiddling with the books."

"No, I didn't but I guess that fills in some blanks. It seemed like what she was taking in terms of drugs was small time. How much did she get you for?"

There was a pause, it sounded like embarrassment , before he told her. "Upwards of $400,000."

Francie gave a long whistle. "How was it that you didn't notice that much was missing? Not to make you feel guilty or anything?"

"No, no, you're quite right, I should have been keeping a better eye on things. But most of that money was supposed to be going into an investment account, an emergency fund that was supposed to be my retirement, and I just never thought about it much, since I was getting my congressional salary."

"Are they going to be able to get it back for you? Her property should be worth twice that?"

"The district attorney said I needed to file a civil action, but they froze her assets so I should recover it, maybe with interest, too."

"Oh, good, then I won't feel guilty about my bill."

He laughed again, "But the big thing is that she is gone," he sighed deeply, "and I can't thank you enough. For me, Doctor Barrett, and our patients."

"I'm glad for you, Doc, and glad to get those two off the street. No telling what harm they might have done."

He thanked her again and they ended their call. Francie got up from her desk and went into the kitchen where she put on the kettle to make a cup of tea. While she stood at the counter, waiting for the water to boil, she looked across her living area and out the big glass windows toward the ocean. Her mind traveled over time and space, as the conversation with Doc Hardwicke had produced completion for the case.

She was pleased with the resolution, of course, for herself and for her client. She even did her best to wish that the Adlers would get some help in prison, though with all of the budget cuts, that seemed unlikely. Maybe they'd find religion and wouldn't be so dangerous when they got out, but Francie made a note to herself to call the DA so she would be notified when they were to be released.

The kettle whistled, and brought her back with a smile.

*   *   *   *   *

The smile wasn't about the tea. Francie remembered a ticket (sic) to resolving her issues with LuxAir. She clacked away at the computer, digging through ancient files, to come across her Washington phone list. And there, sure enough, was the name and number that could bring her relief. Bella Moriarty was a young lobbyist for the organization that represented the wishes of the airline industry to Congress. Francie had called her a couple of times when she was working on stories involving the airline industry or the local airports. She had found the woman to always be honest with her – something quite rare among lobbyists – and Francie had always been straight with her.

She was still at the same number. "Bella, a voice from the past."

"Francie, how great to hear from you," she said in a voice that echoed her words. Caller ID was a wonderful thing; Francie had called her on her business line which was set up to reveal that it was she who was calling. It was necessary for her clients who screened their incoming calls.

"How's life in the Beltway?"

"Hah! As bad as ever. I keep saying that I'll get out, but I've been dating a Congressman from the Houston area for the last three years, and I couldn't imagine that being my other choice."

"Smart girl. If it's not the heat and humidity down there, it's the pollution from all those refineries."

"Yeah. Plus I don't think they have books down there."

Francie chuckled.

"How's life with you?" she asked. "Still doing journalism?"

"No, I left that. Had a stint in the San Francisco market and they wanted me to get a boob job to keep my contract."

"Oh my god, you're kidding?"

"The news director was a real dope, as well as a perv. I was running my tape recorder when he offered the, um, deal. They settled out of court."

"Good for you," Bella said enthusiastically. "One for the good guys."

"And good gals," she told her. "So now I'm a consulting detective, working a little, loving the Monterey Peninsula. Having a wonderful life, actually."

"Oh, Francie, I'm so pleased for you. Do you need an assistant? I'm experienced at climbing through the muck."

That was an interesting idea, and Francie's silence underscored its significance to the other end of the call. "Hmm," she said. "We should think about that."

"Really? Oh, that would be great," the woman said. "I know, I know, lots to talk about but I have to tell you I feel like someone just threw me a lifeline. Even if no. Thank you for that. Now there's hope."

"You're a dear, Bella, and perhaps this is a most fortuitous call," she told her.

"Oh my goodness, how selfish of me, Francie. Certainly that's not why you called," she effused.

Francie laughed, "Maybe it was. But let me tell you why I thought I was calling." And she outlined her situation with LuxAir. When she finished she could almost hear Bella shaking her head three thousand miles away.

"It's quite sad, isn't it, that the customer service is so awful," she said. "Not just the airlines, of course, but it seems epidemic these days. So is the news for that matter. They're not serving the public."

"Yep," Francie agreed. "That's why I'm out here by the ocean, and on the aikido mat three days a week. And only taking cases that are of interest to me, where I can make a difference."

"Ooh, please tell me there's enough work for two."

"You know, there probably is."

"Sorry, I got distracted. I think I could hear the waves in the background." They both laughed. "Are you near the ocean, Francie?"

"Seventy-five feet horizontal, twenty-five feet vertical, depending on the tides."

"That's close. Do you worry about tsunamis?"

"Not for a minute. As Eva Peron said, when asked if she was

frightened when they found a bomb on her plane – they had evacuated the passengers first – 'No one dies five minutes before the time God has set for them.'"

"I like that."

Francie could hear her digesting the thought.

"Francie, I'll take care of the miles thing myself. Give me your frequent flyer number, please."

She did. And they exchanged email addresses.

"Good, good. I'll send a confirming email. Then check your account and let me know, if you would, that it worked. I don't foresee a problem."

"Marvelous, Bella. As Rick told Captain Renault, I think this is the beginning of a beautiful friendship."

*   *   *   *   *

Author's Note: The first Francie LeVillard story to be posted online at MontereyMystery.com was "Doc," and the first episode went up on December 1ˢᵗ 2011. That day there was a major police action on the main drag in Monterey. This was most unusual as Monterey is normally a quiet town.

It turned out that someone had held up a pharmacy and demanded drugs. Morphine and OxyContin. The perp had then run into a café next door and locked himself in the bathroom. The cops tried to talk him out but had no success. After three hours, they heard a crashing sound, and broke down the door to find the man borderline comatose. He must have ingested something. They got him to the hospital but he died.

When I called the local newspaper and informed them of the amazing coincidence, they wrote up the story as a sidebar to their front page coverage of the actual news.

The (Monterey) Herald, December 2, 2011

Monterey writer launches online mystery

Local writer Tony Seton unveiled his new online detective serial at www.Monterey Mystery.com on Thursday. It details a doctor's office contending with patients stealing pharmaceuticals, namely OxyContin and Vicodin.

In a coincidence, Monterey County law enforcement dealt with a real-life pharmaceutical thief suspect in Downtown Monterey on the same day (See story on page A1).

"When the call came in from a friend about the robbery attack on the Ordway Pharmacy, it seemed like truth was indeed stranger than fiction," said Seton.

Monterey Mystery.com tells the story of Francie LeVillard, a consulting detective in the style of Sherlock Holmes.

In the premier, LeVillard is asked to help a doctor deal with the theft of Vicodin and OxyContin from his office.

New episodes will post the first and 15th of each month.

As for the coincidence, Seton wanted to put any suspicions to rest, lest a real-life detective get on his case.

"For the record," Seton said," this episode was written in September.

Marc Cabrera can be reached at 646-4345 or at mcabrera@monterey herald.com.

The Francie LeVillard Mysteries

A House Divided

Her name is Francie LeVillard. She is the great-grand-daughter of a French police detective who worked with Sherlock Holmes. She must have some of his genes because she is a consulting detective, in the style of Holmes. She's pushing forty, is near five-seven, with decent features and dark hair. She takes good care of herself, training in aikido three times a week and walking by the ocean a lot; she lives just south of the Carmel Highlands. A writer friend of hers described her as "bright, attractive, and bad news to the bad guys." She laughed when she heard it, but the description worked for her.

Her parents were liberal Democrats, but unlike Alex Keaton in *Family Ties* she followed their track. It wasn't because they were her parents, but because she believed in the essential principles of goodness, integrity, and making sure that the concept of earning a living didn't leave anyone out of the living part. After covering politics as a reporter in New York and Washington for over a decade, she got pretty jaded about all politicians, liberal Democrats included. While some of them walked the talk, they were very few in number and those were largely ineffective.

So she had her doubts that the greatest democracy in the world could actually continue to function as such. Especially since it seemed that everyone on Capitol Hill, regardless of party, was in the pockets of some industry or another. Was it nobler to take millions from organized labor than from the corporations they battled? Initially maybe, but when they just sat there gridlocked for decades on end while the middle class evaporated and the corporate titans got rich beyond obscene, then no.

Francie still voted, of course, but it was all too often with Molly Ivins' description in mind, that the choice in 2008 was "the evil of two lessers." She was not happy with Obama, but she thought McCain was kinda crazy, and Palin made him look good. The next election saw the donkeys look like asses as the neo-cons surged to the fore. Less than a year in, the 112th Congress had a nine percent approval rating, and no one could figure out why it was that high.

Actually, sarcasm didn't begin to describe the nation's mood which was somewhere between fury and fear. Not a healthy spot for a democracy, but reflective of the fact that Washington – and Sacramento, for that matter – seemed to be on another planet. Francie had gone through her discouraged stage, and now was sitting back on her heels, her journalist's hat hanging in the closet, watching as history wrote itself. There was nothing else to be done.

That sets the background for this story, both of Francie and her political leanings, and here's the tale.

One day recently Francie was in Carmel, getting a new cartridge for her fountain pen at Bittner's, when a woman she sorta knew called out to her and hurried over to collar Francie before she could escape.

"Francie, my dear," effused Delilah Dyce, "Oh my goodness,

how long has it been?"

The answer that was biting Francie's lips to get out gracefully morphed into a smile. That didn't stop the woman. In fairness, Delilah wasn't a bad person, but she could be a nuisance. She was busy morning, noon, and night as a volunteer for a half-dozen local do-gooder organizations, soliciting contributions, herding volunteers, setting up silent auctions, et cetera. Her problem was that she seemed to be under the impression that everyone shared her sentiments, and that it was her job to get as much time and money out them as she could, until they dropped.

The obvious defense against Dyce and her ilk was to not answer emails or phone calls. This was Francie's strategy, and it would have been flawless if she had remained in her house all the time, but alas...

"You simply must come to the event tomorrow night, you simply must."

"I'm busy tomorrow, Dee," Francie replied easily, but some little voice in the back of her head said it wasn't going to be so easy.

"Oh, I mean tonight, it's tonight," the woman said, laughing gayly. "Tomorrow it's the animals, tonight it's this absolutely marvelous man. Oh my goodness, if I could only afford to divorce Maynard, but, anyway... He's married. Gorgeous wife."

"Ah," was all Francie could manage.

"Franklin Hayes is going to be at the Beach Club tonight." Delilah cocked her head back. "You're single, I know you're single..." She thought for a moment – that was her limit – and then repeated herself, "But anyway, he's married. Gorgeous wife."

Thinking she was off the hook, Francie ventured. "Who is Franklin Hayes?" It was a mistake she would never make again. You can never encourage these people, or even leave an opening. Being polite didn't count with such a protagonist.

"Who is Franklin Hayes?" she echoed. "Why my dear Francie, he's only the most wonderful political hope of our time."

There was so much fervor pouring out of her Francie thought she was going to faint. At least that would give her time to get away, but the woman hung in there. "I thought we voted for hope in oh-eight," Francie said between her teeth.

"Oh no, dear, he was a Democrat. Franklin Hayes is a Republican." She grimaced. "Well, sort of. The Republicans wouldn't let him run on their ticket, so he's running as an independent. Stupid Republicans. They haven't had such an attractive candidate in thirty years. And I don't mean just good-looking. Franklin Hayes is smart and funny, and he makes sense."

"Why didn't the Republican party like him?" Francie asked hesitantly, her curiosity piqued.

"Oh, silly things. Social issues."

"Which social issues?"

Delilah lowered her voiced, "The man is pro-choice, he says gay people should be able to marry if they want, and he says the illegal alien immigrants should be given a way to become Americans...you know, in a while."

"I can see why the Republicans didn't like him," Francie said without smiling.

"Not only that, he says we should bring all of our troops home. You know, get out of Afghanistan and those other places."

"Holy moly," Francie returned. "Next you're going to tell me he thinks the rich should have to pay higher taxes."

That stopped her. "So you do know about him?"

"No, Dee, I was just fishing. Does he really?"

"Well, yes, but maybe he'll get over it. I mean, he's very wealthy. Surely he doesn't want his money to go to the government who will just hand it out to the welfare queens."

"When is this thing, Dee?"

She almost did faint then. "You mean you might come?"

"Maybe," Francie allowed.

"Seven-thirty at the Beach Club," she said, clearly delighted. She knew maybe meant yes. Francie was a get, as they say in booking circles; a get that had made her day.

*   *   *   *   *

If the Beach Club at Pebble Beach is on your bucket list – a place you want to visit before you shuffle off this mortal coil – try to go a half-hour before sunset, on a day when the fog remains far out at sea. The BC has lots of windows facing south and west that offer marvelous vistas over Carmel Bay. This was one of those beautiful evenings around the Ides of March.

Francie was surprised at the range of people in

attendance. There were probably a hundred people, a mix of men and women, and ages from late teens to seventies. What was startlingly common about most of those she saw was that they showed a light on. Their brains were working. They were there for political rather than social reasons.

She parked herself at the end of the bar furthest from the entrance so she could observe. That was the journalist in her; the observer rather than the participant. She recognized a number of faces as she scanned the room and watched the door. And she picked the mind of Billy the bartender, who had been observing in this room for most of three decades.

First, though, they did their "it's-been-a-long-time" dance. A largish fellow with a wide grey mustache, he looked genuinely pleased to see her. In truth, he was genuinely pleased to see most people. That's the way he felt about life. "Hello, Miss Francie," he said.

"Hello, Billy. Forget how to pronounce my last name?"

"Miss Villard," he said evenly but pronouncing the l's.

"Close. I think 'Miss Francie' is just fine. Or just Francie. I call you Billy, after all."

"I can call you Francie?"

"I'd be honored, Billy."

"Francie it is...Francie." He dropped two maraschino cherries in her vodka tonic and placed it on a cocktail napkin on the bar in from of her.

"You remembered," she said with great pleasure.

"I never forget a drink," he said and they both laughed.

"So what do you know about this crowd?" she asked, looking back at the growing numbers.

"Not sure. I've heard a little talk about this guy Hayes." He raised his eyebrows. "Most of it's been favorable. The only negative is they say he can't win."

"Hmm. Why can't he win?"

"Because he's too left for the Republicans, and there's no way the Democrats are going to force Feinstein out. At least that's what I heard."

"Someone told me today that he's running as an independent."

"Yeah, good luck. When was the last time an independent won?"

Francie shrugged. "Does he have any money?"

"Yep, tons of it. He designed some kind of resistor or chip or something that everyone uses. Not as rich as Bill Gates or that Ellison guy, but it's at least a couple of billion."

"Hmm," Francie said again. "Whitman spent what, $142 million of her own money, when she lost to Brown."

"Yeah, and she made more than that during the campaign on her investments," Billy said. Francie had forgotten how well he kept himself up on the news.

"Is this guy like that? Like Whitman?"

"No, not from what I've heard. He's apparently a

good guy. He's not put on. And he's got a sense of humor. According to what I pick up here at the bar."

"A sense of humor is good."

At that point they were interrupted by the room breaking into applause. Not the raucous kind, but polite and respectful. This was Pebble Beach after all, even though many of the people in the room were from elsewhere. The applause, of course, marked the arrival of the candidate. He walked comfortably through the crowd and stepped up onto a single riser and turned to faced them.

Hayes was maybe a bit on the small side; not a football player. He looked a healthy forty-ish, with neat brown hair, a light tan complexion on a round-ish face and slightly narrowed eyes. He wore nice slacks, a quiet shirt and tie, and a light grey corduroy sports jacket.

What was amazing, if you've ever been to such a function, was that there was no gratuitous intro-duction. The guy whom the people in the room had come to see and hear was there to speak to them. (Another thing about not being introduced is that you don't have to go through a bunch of thank-you's.) Franklin Hayes just launched into his remarks.

"I don't want to go to Washington. I love it here." He pointed to the setting sun sparkling on the water. "Who wouldn't?" The audience rippled with its agreement. "But I think I can catalyze a change there. I would have run for the House, taking the more traditional route, but being one of one hundred – the winner of a major upset election – would give me more voice than being one of 435.

"So I would like to lay out my ideas for you, and if you like what you hear – if you agree that what I'm talking about is the America you want – then I will leave it in your hands to rouse your friends and relatives to go to the polls and vote for a new way of doing things. I don't pretend that my election alone will do the trick, but I think when other states see what we have done, the ball will get rolling quickly, in the right direction.

"I don't know why any of you are here, other than you heard from someone else that this would be worth your while. They were right. Here's why. People think we have a two-party system. We don't. It's one party. The Democrats and the Republicans have all been drinking from the same poisoned well of special-interest politics. They are about their re-election first, and then protecting their party. Our nation is down on the list of importance to them.

"And no wonder. The lobbyists invest millions of dollars in their campaigns. The politicians have been bought and paid for.

"Maybe you'll think when you hear my platform that I should have run as a Republican. They wouldn't have me. I'm not one of them.

"But I'm not because I'm a true conservative, and most Republicans today are not, despite what they say and what the media parrots about them.

"The major principles of true conservatives are conservation, a balanced budget, personal responsibility, and no foreign wars. That doesn't sound like today's Republicans. Does it? It sounds a lot like Teddy Roosevelt though.

"But when you hear the Republicans now, they scoff at climate change and support subsidies for oil, coal, and nuclear. That's about as far from conservation as you can get.

"The Republicans today are obsessing about reducing the deficit, but they were the ones who pushed through the trillions of dollars of the Bush tax cuts for the wealthiest and now they're insisting that those tax cuts be made permanent."

Francie and Billy both listened to the speaker. He wasn't captivating, but he was engaging. He didn't sound like a politician, for one thing. He wasn't pulling punches, he was just laying out the facts as he saw them, and they were far different from the mind-numbing talking points that Dems and Reps spouted.

Hayes spoke about the scourge of party politics that had grid-locked the government. He called for a massive shift of research funds from military projects to solar power, and to rebuilding our infrastructure. Beyond the details, which clearly pleased the audience, he spoke directly, not like the snake-oil hucksters who flooded the cable airwaves with mean lies and false promises. He wasn't a cheerleader and they weren't a group of fans. So when he called for bringing home all American troops, and instituting a single-payer health care system, the people listening and watching didn't interrupt with cheers. They gave him their respectful attention.

"That's what I'm about. That's the kind of thinking I want to instigate in Washington. It may seem pie-in-the-sky, but if we don't remember what's important – and push for it – then the special interests will win.

Even more than they already have. They will bankrupt our country, financially and morally." He paused and then said, "Thank you. Now I invite your comments and questions."

Applause began and rose to a clamor. Francie turned to Billy. "What'd you think?"

"If he could do half of what he said, I'd have hope for our country again."

Francie nodded her head in agreement.

"Shhh," Franklin Hayes had his hands up, trying to quiet the crowd. "Please, I appreciate your applause, but let's put that energy into rounding up the votes we need to get this going." Then he started taking questions. Most were about policy rather than politics, and the candidate gave short, clear answers that satisfied the askers. After fielding more than a dozen questions, Hayes thanked the audience again, stepped down onto the floor and started mingling, shaking hands, listening before talking.

As the would-be senator mixed with the crowd, Francie turned back to Billy and they talked quietly about what they'd heard. Both were impressed. Francie watched Hayes' reflection in the mirror behind the bar and noticed that he moved invariably in their direction.

It was a few minutes later that Hayes arrived at the bar. He said hello to Billy and they shook hands. Then he turned and introduced himself to Francie.

"I think you're Francie LeVillard," he said, pronouncing her name so perfectly she couldn't help herself and turned to smile at Billy. Billy was an intuitive fellow, and he moved away. It wasn't her smile; he just knew that Hayes had come to speak with her.

"That would be I," she agreed, holding her drink in her right hand and making no move to put it down to shake his. She could see that he was processing that piece of information.

"I was hoping to meet you. I've heard a lot of good things about you."

"Really?" she said. "I hadn't heard about you until I ran into Delilah Dyce this morning, most propitiously it seems. I liked what you had to say. Have you been campaigning long?"

He shook his head. "Not in public. Just small groups, organized by friends. I wanted to make sure that I wasn't deluding myself about what the country really wants."

"And you're not?" she asked, her eyebrows raised. "That's why you're here tonight?"

Hayes smiled at her. "Yes, it's my first group of this size. Mostly arranged by Delilah and a few mutual friends. On just a couple of days notice. It happened that the Beach Club had a party booked that was cancelled."

"It's a good sign when things line up for you. Sort of an affirmation for what you're doing."

"I hadn't thought about it in those terms exactly, but I think you are right."

"Were you pleased with your delivery and your reception?"

He smiled again. Francie had taken him up a level. "Both, actually. What did you think?"

She took a long sip of her drink, and then told him, "I thought you did well and the audience appreciated you."

"And?"

"And if they weren't more enthusiastic, it's because they're more upscale than most audiences you will be addressing. Also, many of these people I suspect invested a lot of hope in Barack Obama and have been disappointed."

"And you?"

"Yes, I've been disappointed, not only by him, but also the total lack of leadership in the Congress. It is a black hole of progress."

"I meant, did you like what I had to say?"

She took another sip of her drink and then smiled at him. "I didn't realize how large the chasm was between Republicans and true conservatives. That was a big deal for me. I like those values. But I've always thought I was a progressive. Well, since I got fed up with the liberals. I wonder how you characterize yourself, politically I mean."

He chuckled. "I think maybe I'm a progressive conservative."

She chuckled back. "That fits."

"Miss LeVillard," he began. They both knew he'd come over to speak to her for a reason. It wasn't just a how-did-I-do encounter.

"Mr. Hayes," she replied.

"I wonder if we might get together for a cup of coffee at your convenience."

"Might I ask the purpose of such a meeting?"

"I'd rather discuss it privately. Entirely professional, of course. I'm in need of someone with your skills as a consulting detective."

Francie didn't show it, but it pleased her that he had dug deeply enough, not only to know how to pronounce her name, but also to distinguish her as a consulting detective. She peered at him for what might have seemed like a long time. She wasn't really looking at the man, but beyond him, out to where ideas come from.

*   *   *   *   *

They met two mornings later at Pastries and Petals, a delightful little restaurant on the north side of Carmel. The coffee was good; the food was delicious. Francie had suggested ten o'clock because it would be between the breakfast and lunch crowds. In fact there was only a table of four older ladies who might have already put in a couple of hours together, but the other tables were empty. Arriving first, Francie snagged a table for two and sat on the padded bench with her back against the wall. She didn't like to have her back exposed if she could avoid it. She'd crossed too many miscreants, and they weren't all in prison, or dead.

Franklin Hayes arrived only three minutes late, but he apologized, declaring, gracefully, his distaste for the perverted quaint notion that the City of Carmel-by-the-Sea had of not numbering buildings. Francie nodded sympathetically, having long thought it was ridiculous that street numbers were considered a sign of civilization's collapse, a notion which defenders of the status quo held to their bosom like the most evangelical crusaders.

She had waited to order, and then chosen coffee and a pastry, appropriately. Hayes had the same. The food and drink before them, she waited for him to explain why he had asked to meet with her. It was quite a wait. He sipped his coffee and ate his cherry tart before he thought to get down to business. He sat back in his chair and gave her a long look. It seemed like a control game to her and she didn't like games.

"I bill at $500 an hour, or fraction thereof," she told him. While it was true, she said it more to make a point.

He laughed and said, "Yes, and from what I hear, you are worth it. I'm glad to pay." He leaned forward and tilted his head slightly. "I want you on my team," he said with a firm smile, and repeated, "I want you on my team."

Francie looked to her left and to her right, as though wondering whom he was addressing. Then she chuckled and asked, "Whatever do you mean?"

He was slightly disquieted by her response. "I want you to be my security chief."

Francie tilted her head to show that she didn't quite

get what he was talking about.

"I want you to manage security for my campaign."

"Why would you think I should do that?"

She thought she detected a hint of irritation, and maybe that was what he was feeling. She couldn't blame him if he thought that she was toying with him; she was.

He steadied himself. "I did my homework. I know that you're the best on The Peninsula." He gave her the opportunity to acknowledge the remark but she passed. "You are not only bright – and particularly intuitive – but you have a systems approach. You can find things that are out of alignment where others can't."

Francie wondered to whom he had been talking and where he had gotten that assessment, because while it was true, she wasn't aware that any of her clients, past or present, would have described her in those terms.

"What kind of security do you think you need? This isn't a bodyguard thing, I presume."

"No, no, no...it's about the campaign operation. I sense that there might be a leak. I'm not sure. It's more a feeling. I would like to have confidence in my staff, and not worry about things said in my office being given to the media or my opponents."

"You already have a staff? Of course you should, I just didn't realize that you were that far along."

"I have a core group of four. I assembled the group as of two weeks ago, when the response I got was what

I was looking for, and I determined that I should move forward. They all have campaign experience. They all are unhappy with the political scene today. They are excited about my ideas and purpose. Two are Republicans, two are Democrats."

"And you think one of them might not be fully on your side?"

"I don't know that. It seems unlikely. Drat, I sound like a fool. But I have this feeling that...well, it's like you feel a breeze but you don't see a window open."

"Drat?" Francie laughed. "I like that. I have a friend who does security of the kind that you probably need. She can check out your computers and your phones, and put traps in the email system. She's very good. She's worked with some of the top federal operations as a consultant."

Hayes looked at her with an expression of disappointment. "That's not what I'm looking for. I'm asking you to tell me if I'm wrong about feeling that there is a soft spot in my operation. This isn't electronic. It's intuitive."

"Ah."

"Miss LeVillard, I suppose I sound impatient, but I know what I want and you're it. I knew when I saw you at the Beach Club. It confirmed what I had heard about you. I'm not being petulant because I must have what I want. It's just that I know you would be right for me and I think you do, too, so I don't understand why you are resisting me."

"My resistance, Mr. Hayes, is that I don't like politics. I am impressed by what you said the other night. I think our country would be in a lot better shape if there were a couple of hundred like you on Capitol Hill." She stopped there.

"But?"

Francie wondered how to answer his question. Sarah came over and topped their coffee cups, giving her a little more time to think.

"Okay," she said simply.

That surprised him. "Okay? What does that mean? You'll do it?" He realized that was what she meant.

She nodded.

"Great," he said, his voice a mixture of relief and enthusiasm.

She held up a palm toward him. "But it has to be done my way."

"Sure," he said quickly, and then frowned slightly and asked, "What does that mean?"

"It means that you pay me directly. It doesn't come through the campaign."

"Okay," he agreed.

"And there is no publicity about my working for you."

That was a surprise to him. "Why not? It would be great PR for the campaign, and it would set you well in the community."

"I'm not interested in publicity. In fact, I shy away from it. It's not good for the work that I do. I think you must have inferred that from the lack of citations you found when you googled me."

He nodded. "Very little current."

"That's by my choice. I don't need business. I particularly don't need clients who want to accessorize with a high-profile consultant. It's especially a plague among politicians who try to wrap up the best campaign consultants, simply to keep them out of the enemy's camp. That's not the same with me since I stay away from politics, but if you want me to work with you – with you, not for you – then you must accept that I can be most effective doing so my way, quietly."

"All right," he said, more with digestion than reluctance. He reached inside his coat pocket and pulled out a piece of paper. When he reached for a pen, he came up empty. He saw her pen by her notebook on the table. "May I borrow your pen, please?"

"No," she said easily. Then she called Sarah over from behind the counter. "May he borrow a pen, please, Sarah?"She pulled one from her apron and handed it to Hayes.

He made some scribblings on the piece of paper, folded it, returned it to his pocket, and put the pen on the table. He smiled at me. "Is that pen special?"

"Yes. No one writes with it but me."

"Why is that, if I may ask?"

"Sure. A friend of mine, Tony Seton, is a writer, and he got a pen like this. When I asked to try it, he looked at me askance. He said something like,

'Certainly not' as though he was shocked that I might even ask. Then he realized that he had to explain. He said he'd been looking for the right pen for the nearly five decades that he'd been paid for his writing. It wasn't that he did his work long hand, but rather, it was an icon for him. He'd tried various pens over the years. He'd tried expensive pens and not, ballpoints, flow-tips, fountain, and cartridge pens. There was a time when he mixed his own inks.

"But he never was happy with the results. Five years ago maybe, he decided he would never find the right instrument. He thought it ironic, and ridiculous, as well he might. And then a couple of months ago, he was chatting up Detlef Bittner – he has the pen store over on Ocean – and Detlef showed him the Pilot Vanishing Point Retractable Fountain Pen, and he fell in love with it. Tony told me to try it out – not his but one at Bittner's place – and I fell in love with it. I never enjoyed writing as much that I can remember."

Francie laughed. "More than you wanted to know, of course, but maybe that gives you a sense of whom you're dealing with. You can still back out."

Hayes chuckled. "Not on your life. Please send me an invoice for your retainer, and let me know how you want to proceed." Then he stood up and seemed ready to go. But first he looked down at Francie. "Good," he said, and then turned and left.

Francie remained seated. She scanned her mind for a fresh check of this new client. She usually could raise some questions in her mind but in this case, she realized, he seemed whole to her. There could be problems – there were always curve balls – but she was pleased with the results of her first meeting with Franklin Hayes.

*   *   *   *   *

Francie wasn't to get involved right away. As it happened she had a couple of matters to deal with out of state. But that was fine since the campaign was still in its formative stages. Franklin Hayes was a bright fellow, she knew that already, and he was also very organized in his mind. She liked that. "Call it the Virgo in me," she had once explained to a friend, "but I like things to work, and not everyone is designed to both envision and implement."

Hayes was planning to open his first campaign headquarters at the upscale Crossroads Carmel shopping center. It was a matter of convenience, and the address, as it happened, was a good metaphor. Hayes held a lease on a space where the previous tenants had opened a bookstore but hadn't really known what they were doing. It was not atypical in this area, where there were a lot of people who had money, and spouses who needed something to do.

Francie had arranged for Ariane Chevasse, whom she fondly referred to as "my spook friend" because she was into security and intelligence issues, to oversee the technical side of the security at the new headquarters. Ariane was not only a pro, but also a close friend. They had met on the aikido mat, where they both now trained. Ariane was born in America to French parents, and from their influence and a number of lengthy visits to the country, she had become such a Francophile that she spoke her native language with a French accent.

Ariane was remarkably well-connected, and she and Francie had been involved in several significant cases that are too sensitive still to recount. Considering what she had been involved with at the top levels of government and private industry, this job at the Hayes campaign headquarters was basically a favor to her friend. Plus, Ariane had the time because she was between larger gigs, and she enjoyed playing with the latest toys on someone else's tab.

She designed the phone and computer networks for the office plus their external interface, and she established protocols for email and cellphone use. She had discussed the controls with Francie who had asked her to set it up so that, as the campaign security consultant, she would have access to everything. Only Hayes would also have the tier-one control.

*   *   *   *   *

Her initial reason for going to Ohio was rather obscure. She had been at a lecture on understanding death put on by the Unity Church in Monterey a few weeks earlier. The point of the lecture was that there was a likelihood of existence after a person's body dies. The lecturer had given a reasonable nod to the ecclesiastical views of heaven but focused his talk on the non-theistic view that had to do with the soul as energy that was part of a universal life force. His point was that what life meant in relation to what came after it basically came down to the personal responsibility that a person exercised during his stay on Earth.

It was a reasonably interesting lecture, though most of the material was familiar to Francie. She had attended with a friend who hadn't been doing too well emotionally and could benefit, she humbly had thought, from a different world view, specifically one that would edge her out of her victimhood drone.

At least that's why she had thought she was going to the event. Because then as they were walking out the door, an older man – he looked older than he probably was, by years; she guessed early sixties – stopped her on the stairs. He was bald, with the weathered face of someone who'd spent a lot of time outside, probably in the southern states. He was neatly dressed, and wore a slightly confused expression.

"Excuse me, you are Miss LeVillard?" he asked in a voice that featured an unmistakable Chicago origin.

"Yes, I am."

"I'm sorry to bother you, but I've heard about you, and read some in the papers, and I think I would like to consult with you."

She was about to say something but he started again quickly.

"Oh no, I don't mean here, not now. I want to make an appointment."

Francie's friend tapped her on the arm, said "Thank

you," and walked away.

Francie was about to speak to the man, but again he jumped in.

"I have money, you don't have to worry about that. I can pay. I can pay."

"You didn't tell me your name," Francie suggested gently.

He gave a short laugh, "Oh yeah right. I guess I'm surprised that I run into you. I was in the back of the lecture when I saw you and I thought maybe – like the speaker said about coincidence – that I should take advantage of it." He abruptly held out his hand. "Larry Milverton."

It was a weathered paw that felt a little arthritic. Or it could have been due to injuries or just hard work. Her guess was construction.

"How do you do?"

"I'm all right, you know, but I have a situation and I'd like to talk about it with someone who is smart. I know you're smart, but I mean, it's the kind of smart that I think you can help me."

"All right," she told him, sensing that it was a situation with more import than she might have thought. "Is this an urgent matter?"

"I guess it is," he said thoughtfully. "I'm dying, you know, and I have to clean something up. Not bad. Just make it right."

She agreed that they should meet for coffee the next morning at ten. She suggested the East Village but he didn't like the idea. "Too many of those people out front, you know."

She did know. There was an unfortunate gathering of the unwashed in a little plaza area in front of the coffee house. Most were probably not dangerous, or even criminals, but there was a lot of smoking – cigarettes – loud swearing, and general discouragement.

"How 'bout Parisian Bakery?" he countered.

"The Paris Bakery is a favorite place of mine," she replied with a smile. "See you tomorrow morning at ten."

He nodded and moved away.

Francie told herself as she watched him walk slowly up the sidewalk and out of sight that she really had to make more of an effort to screen out her presumptions about people, especially notions that were based on dress, or style of talking. Time after time her presumptions were wrong, both ways. Some folks who were very cultured in appearance and presentment were very crude in their thinking, while some with a less polished exterior had the most refined souls.

In Larry Milverton's case, as she discovered the next morning, he wasn't a customer of the Paris Bakery, but he'd been in Monterey and the environs for ten years, and knew of it. He thought it would be appropriate for her.

She was right about one thing; his accent. He was from Chicago. He had left The Windy City when he was 19. He never got along with his parents, and he had had to escape. She was right about another thing. He had hopped the bus and headed for the Florida Panhandle, where he worked in construction for the next thirty years. He had lived very frugally and put away most of what he earned.

Then there'd been an accident – not his fault – and he had suffered permanent nerve damage in his right hand. He couldn't use tools any more. With a decent worker's comp payoff, he decided he'd had enough of Florida and wanted to try the West Cost. He drove to Los Angeles, discovered immediately that it wasn't his cup of tea and headed north, taking I-5 all the way up to Redding.

"That's wasn't for me either. I'd spent the last thirty years with rednecks, and that was why I left. Redding had a lot of the same kind of people. You know, always blaming big government but always first in line to get their government checks."

So back in the car, he drove back south, skipping the Bay Area, which he knew wasn't for him, and down to Santa Cruz.

"It was all right, you know, but a little, what would you say, dark maybe. I liked this end of The Bay better." He found himself a tiny in-law unit in Pacific Grove and had been there since. Six months before he'd met Francie on the church steps, he'd been diagnosed with an inoperable brain tumor. The prognosis had been maybe a year, and so he didn't think he'd probably be around much longer.

"Not this lifetime anyway," he said, with an empty laugh. "That's why I was at that seminar yesterday, you know. Checking things out. Maybe figure out where I'm going, if you know what I mean." He stood up without saying anything and brought their coffee cups over to the counter to be refilled. Then he returned, putting their cups down before he regained his seat.

"The coffee's pretty good here, don't you think?"

Francie agreed.

"The reason why I wanted to consult with you was that when I left Chicago, I was glad to be away from my parents, my mother especially; she was mean. But there was also a situation with my sister that I've got to tell you about. And it's what I want you to help me fix, and I think you can.

"My sister was five years older, and she and I were really close growing up. We kinda protected each other from our mother. But anyway, she started seeing this guy and it wasn't like he turned her away from me, it's just that he took her up time, you know. They had a relationship. And I didn't think it was right 'cause he was a priest, and they aren't supposed to, you know, have relationships.

"So I was really lost without my sister. And I got to feeling really angry and I did something really bad. I told some people that the priest had like, you know, molested me." He sighed deeply. The pain was clear in his expression. "He didn't, but I told some people, and the word got out. And when the bishop asked me to come and see him, I said it didn't matter. I wasn't gonna press charges or anything."

"Was it true? Were you molested?"

He shook his head. "No. I was trying to stop him

from seeing my sister, so I could have her." He hurriedly added, "Not in that way, I mean so we could be friends again. I thought they would force him to stop seeing her. But instead, he left the church. My sister told me she hated me and never wanted to see me again, but the priest – well, he wasn't a priest anymore – he told her that she had to forgive me.

"And maybe she did, but I couldn't stay there anymore. I was so angry, you know, with myself. With what I had done. Plus my mother was making me feel even worse, so I just took off."

Francie thought she might have an idea where this was going, but pushed the speculation out of her head. She knew she could be wrong, again, so what was the point?

"So like I told you, I went to Florida, and I never got in touch with them again. I thought they would be better off never talking to me again. It was so long ago, now, I don't know if they even remember me." He picked up his cup and sipped his coffee.

"So this is what happened now. I saw in the paper a story about this guy, who left Chicago around the same time as me, and in the story it said that his family thought maybe he had been murdered. That was when the cops started digging up the house John Wayne Gacy had. He killed all those young men. More than thirty of 'em, and they didn't identify all of them. So this guy, his family thought maybe he was one of those people, but they did a DNA test and it wasn't so they looked for him and they found him. In Texas, I think.

"So I was thinking, maybe my sister thought I was

one of those bodies they found under the guy's house. That really bothered me. I didn't want her to think that he had, like seduced me, you know, and then murdered me and buried me in the lime. And that's why I wanted you to help me. I want you to find my sister and bring her a letter for me. Tell her that I'm all right, you know, but that I just wanted to tell her that I'm really, really sorry again, and I wanted her to know that."

He looked at Francie for a long moment and then asked, "Would you do that for me? I'll certainly pay you for your time and expenses. Whatever it costs, probably. I'm not going to need money where I'm going, wherever that is."

She looked at him for a while. "I don't usually take this kind of case, Mr. Milverton. I choose to stay away from family matters. But I'll see what I can do for you. I'll see if I can find your sister. At least that."

A smile broke on his face that turned out to wider than Francie thought was possible. Perhaps it was wider than he imagined possible, too. At least since he could remember.

An hour later Francie was on her computer, looking for the sister and the ex-priest. She had no idea if they had stayed together, but since he had left the priesthood for her, it didn't surprise her that she found them together, married, and living in Akron, Ohio. They were running a homeless shelter. When she called Larry Milverton to give him the news, she could hear him fighting back tears. It took him a while to collect himself. Then he asked if she would bring them a letter.

"I'm glad they are together. I've always known that they should be, you know." He laughed. "Maybe I helped by forcing him out of the priesthood." He laughed again. "Anyway, I guess I gotta write something in the letter to him, too." He was silent for a moment. "Will you do it, ma'am? Will you bring them the letter for me? Please?"

"Yes," she said simply. "When will your letter be ready?"

"Today. I'll do it today. I can get it to you today." He was excited, and in a hurry after so many years of not knowing and waiting.

"I checked the airlines. I can leave on Thursday, day after tomorrow. That will give you the time to make your letter say what you want it to say."

When she met him late the next day, he handed her two envelopes, both thin. One had his sister's name on the front. The other had Francie's. He told her that the letter to his sister was a single page. He didn't know what to say to her other than to apologize, which he did several times. The other envelope contained a check for Francie. They had never discussed her fee, but he had more than covered the cost of her time and her expenses.

The next day she flew out of Monterey Regional, one of her favorite airports – it's small, convenient, and the people are less officious – and was soon winging her way eastward.

*   *   *   *   *

It was while Francie was waiting for her connection in Chicago that Ariane called her to say that Hayes' wife had confronted her and demanded a top-level password.

Francie had never met Beth Moriarty, but according to several profile articles she had read about Hayes, his wife had been a corporate lawyer for a Texas oil and gas corporation when she had met her future husband. After they had married, she had quit her job and had three children, who were now seven, nine and eleven. There was no indication in the articles as to what kind of power she wielded in the relationship, nor whether this attempt to insert herself into the campaign was a whim or a warning.

Ariane knew what Francie's answer was but was calling more to inform than confirm. "*Ma chere*, be careful of this one. I think that she is, how do you say, tightly wrapped."

"Aaarrrggghhh," Francie responded.

"That is a word I don't know, I think," Ariane said, laughing, "but I know what you mean. *Oui, c'est dommage*. What can he do, who can he be, if that is his wife?"

"I should have said 'dang'," Francie told her. "You know that word. And you are right. It is not good for the campaign if she is behaving this way. Do you want me to call Hayes?"

"Probably I think you should since it is your arrangement. I told her that I was just your *sous*-contractor. I used my heavy accent to put her off. It is very useful, *tu sais*."

"Yes. It's like people who think they should speak louder to someone who is deaf." They both laughed. When Francie got off the phone with Ariane, she called her client. He had given her a private cell number, but that didn't mean he would always answer it right away. In fact this time, it went into voicemail. Francie didn't deliver important news to clients in a recording; not unless she was through with them. She didn't want to be through with Franklin Hayes.

"Mr. Hayes, this is Francie LeVillard. I am at O'Hare waiting for a connection that leaves in another hour. It's one your time now. Please give me a call when you have a chance. Thank you."

Her phone rang ten minutes later. "Miss LeVillard, Franklin Hayes. My wife says your Miz Chevasse won't give her the password to our security system. What's that about?"

Francie smiled to herself – she liked his efficiency – but her tone was cool. "That's why I was calling, of course. You asked me to be your security consultant. Are you questioning me or canceling the contract?"

That caught him up short. "Questioning...questioning. Not firing."

"Okay," she said, warming slightly. "I didn't want to prolong this if you had changed your mind." She was pretty sure she detected some distress in his mind, not just in his voice, and she didn't think it was about her.

"No, that's right," he replied quickly.

"You need to run a tight ship. You need complete

control over your information flow if your campaign is to have any chance of succeeding. Your opponents are going to try to infiltrate your operation. If you want to prevent that, you have to take precautions that may seem excessive now, but they won't later."

"I understand," he agreed somewhat wearily. He'd made his decision. Now he had to deal with his wife.

"If you want your wife to have the security code, you can give it to her, but I can't provide the kind of control you want if anyone other than you has it."

"Does that mean you don't trust me?" he asked, in a surprisingly light tone.

"No, Mr. Hayes, I think I know you. I don't know your wife, however, and even if I did, you are my client, and I only have one where it comes to a security program. I think you can understand that."

He was quiet for a moment and then he asked, "When do you start calling me Franklin?"

"Probably not until I get back."

She heard him chuckle. "Thanks, uh, Miss LeVillard. Have a good trip."

"Thank you," she told him and clicked off. She was pleased. When a client chose her over a spouse, they knew that their problem was at home, not at the office. Francie would have to keep an eye on him, but she knew how important this senate race was to him, and that's why he was still her client.

*   *   *   *   *

Arriving at the Akron-Canton Airport, Francie got a car and then booked herself into a motel near the terminal. From there she put in a call to Regina Augustus née Milverton. She explained who she was and why she was there. And she asked if she might deliver the letter to her. The sister could have been still angry and then rude to Francie or she could have been happy and relieved. Francie figured that if she had been involved with a priest all these years, and they were doing a noble thing, that it would more likely be the latter response.

"Oh, my goodness, by all means come over. I've been praying for this day for more than forty years. Thank you, thank you, thank you."

Francie had already figured out the directions but let the woman give them to her; she could feel her need to solidify the connection. Fifteen minutes later Francie walked into the clean if humble lobby of their shelter. A large woman came from around the counter, her eyes red, her joy unmistakable. Her features were similar to her brother's but, while older, she was better preserved. She enveloped Francie in her arms and cried some more.

Francie extracted herself from her grasp and steered them over to a long-used couch. When the woman was finally calmed down, Francie took the envelope from her pocket and handed it to her. For a while she just looked at it, her name in his handwriting; there was no return address. Then carefully, she opened the envelope and pulled out the letter. Before opening it she asked Francie, "Have you seen it?" Francie shook her head.

She opened up the letter and held it up, closer to her eyes. Then she read it. Very slowly, judging by her eye movements, and then she read it again. Her hand fell into her lap, holding the letter. She looked out, possibly in the direction of California, her mind a million miles away. A smile grew on her face; so like what Francie had seen on her brother's face two days earlier. She carefully refolded the letter and put it back in the envelope.

"He's sorry," she told Francie. "He's suffered that all these years. He didn't need our forgiveness." She looked at her. "We – Richard and I – were always kind of grateful, for the results, that is, that Richard left the church and we could be together without hiding."

Then came the part that was going to be difficult. "How is my brother? How is Lawrence."

"Did he say anything in the letter?" Francie tried to keep her voice calm.

"No, no. He just spoke about the past, and told me he loved me. That he hoped Richard and me would find it in our hearts to forgive him." Her eyes moistened.

Milverton had told Francie to explain whatever was necessary to make sure that his sister understood how he felt. He said nothing about reuniting, or about his future. That he left up to Francie. Thinking about it on the flight out, she had mulled over esoterically how anyone could set a fee scale for such a task. Not that she was complaining; just thinking about the strange byways of her work. Yes, she thought, just imagine a price list.

Her decision – she'd made it tentatively at 32,000 feet – was to tell his sister everything, and she did, starting with the fact that he seemed to have found great peace after all these years in making contact with his sister. Then what he had told her about his working and traveling and finding just where he wanted to be. She didn't seem surprised at anything Francie told her. Not even when she told the woman that her brother was ill.

"I want to see him," she declared softly. "Before he dies. I will fly out to California. We will. Richard will want to see him, too."

It took Francie a few moments to control her own emotions. "I think that would be very special for him," she told her. "I trust that he gave you his address and phone number?"

She nodded. "Yes he did. Otherwise I would have thought he didn't want to hear from me. But he needs completion, and he shall have it."

She invited Francie to stay with them, to at least have dinner with them, but she declined. She suggested that they might get together when they flew out to see her brother. Francie explained that she had another situation that required her attention, and that she was driving to Columbus in the morning.

*   *   *   *   *

It wasn't a pressing need, calling her to Columbus, but when the Milverton case appeared, it seemed like a good opportunity. Years earlier, when she had shifted from television news to being a consulting detective, her father had asked her if she might learn anything about his half-brother whom he hadn't seen since he was maybe one and Bruce was three. He didn't really remember him, which was no surprise. The boy was the child of Francie's grandfather's first wife. The woman had considerable trouble after the birth. She was depressed, and in such pain that she became addicted to painkillers. She was put in a sanitarium where she stayed for two years. Half-way through, she divorced Francie's grandfather.

That wasn't such a bad thing, as he met and quickly married Francie's grandmother who was a much better fit. She helped to raise the baby, Bruce, as if he were her own child. The child was very happy and thriving, but then the birth mother – or real mother, as they called them back then – got out of the sanitarium and demanded her child be returned to her.

Francie's father told her that his father had urged his ex-wife to let him keep Bruce, that he was in a good home and had a brother, but the woman insisted on taking the boy, and Francie's grandfather decided it would be best not to take the matter to court. Later he wished that he had. A few years later, his ex-wife turned up in the morgue in Albany, and the boy – Francie's half-uncle – had disappeared. The police reported that he had apparently spent most of those years with an aunt of the ex-wife, they thought somewhere in Michigan.

Francie's father wondered if she could possibly find his half-brother, but not to put any serious attention into it. It didn't seem urgent to him, and she was in the midst of matters that were real and urgent, so she asked him if it could wait. He said certainly, and she let it go. Her parents died in a plane crash three months later, and Francie had been burdened by a feeling of guilt ever since. More than the guilt was the fact that as far as she knew, Bruce, if he was still alive, was her only relative.

Francie had mixed feelings about finding him since she had, of course, never known him. For that matter, her father didn't have even fleeting memories of his half-brother; only the stories from his own father. And in truth, theirs was a family that never felt that blood was thicker than water. Maybe it was because the only relatives she had known were her parents, whom she loved, ardently, for who they were as people, which is what mattered more than the fact that they were her father and mother.

That said, when there was a break in the action – and her mind told her it was time – Francie hired a researcher to see what she could find. Francie had her father's DNA chart, so that if she were to find a person who might be her uncle, this would be a way to determine the likelihood of his identity. For the record, Francie's father had left nothing to his half-brother; he had thought he was most likely dead.

As it happened, the researcher found Francie's uncle – or rather his chart – in Columbus. The researcher had reported to her that there were about tens of thousands of unidentified bodies in morgues around the country, and the authorities had been building a data bank of their DNAs before they buried or cremated them. It was a wonderful idea, on many levels, including settling estates and closing cases, although in many situations, there was either no one left, or no one who at least cared about the departed, unless there was an inheritance to be sought.

Francie's uncle Bruce had died two winters earlier. The coroner told her on the phone that he had frozen to death in an aqueduct under a highway bridge on a particularly cold Ohio night. No one had claimed the body. The coroner had registered the DNA and the body had been cremated. Again Francie's feelings were mixed. On the one hand she thought it might have been possible to find him before her parents died, though considering that the discovery had been made through the morgue DNA, that wasn't very likely. People living at that end of society don't have a lot of identity, just invisibility as it were, unless they get into trouble with the police. Her uncle, bless his soul, had no police record.

And on the other hand, Uncle Bruce's departure meant that the case was closed. She thought someone looking into her head might find her response cold. But she argued that she preferred that loose ends be tied up in a way that caused the least disruption to people's lives. This man, who her father hadn't even known – he'd just known of him – died in his sleep, putting a coda to what couldn't have been a happy life, at least not at the end. Nature took her course.

That rational view did not deprive Francie of feelings, and it had been her intention to visit Columbus at some point. The Milverton case brought that point to date. The night she finished with Regina Augustus, she ate lightly and went to bed with a Rex Stout novel. Flying these days was a chore, she thought, and the trip, and its incumbent strains, had caught up with her. She fell asleep with the book on the bed beside her.

Even though her body was on California time, she woke up early, and decided that there was no need wait. She drove to Columbus and there found a place to break her fast while waiting for the coroner's office to open.

The coroner confirmed the information that he had given her on the phone. Then he told her the location of the aqueduct where her uncle's body had been found. He also gave her directions. When she was leaving, he took both of her hands in his and thanked her sincerely for making the effort.

"The time didn't matter, you know? It was the fact that you are here. So few of the people who leave this way through our office have any connections, at least not in our world. It's astounding how many people die anonymously," the coroner told her. "It speaks of their lives, and of those whom they left. I don't get a lot of people asking about them. I appreciate it when I do. Thank you for coming."

Francie left his office and followed the directions to a highway overpass on the edge of the city. As a zillion cars whizzed by above, she walked to the side of the aqueduct and looked down at the place where her Uncle Bruce moved on to his next whatever. There was no trace of anything. There wouldn't be. Not after two years, especially. She wondered how many others had died there, if any.

"Bye, Uncle Bruce," she said aloud. "Good luck." Then she climbed back up to her car and headed north. She had briefly thought about cutting out a leg of her trip by driving to Chicago, but it didn't make sense to spend six hours driving to O'Hare, plus paying the extra charges. She returned to Akron-Canton, and enjoyed her Nero Wolfe story in a remote corner of the airport lounge with little interruption.

*   *   *   *   *

Arriving back in Monterey, when she got home, Francie first thought about calling Larry Milverton. But she realized that his sister would have been in touch with him by this time. She would wait for him to call, as she expected he would. Meantime, there were two messages on her business line from Franklin Hayes, saying how much he was looking forward to her return. She hadn't told him exactly when that would be so she didn't feel any urgency about her returning his call. She checked her email; nothing pressing. She opened a bottle of Hahn 2009 GSM Cabernet, a delicious blend from their vineyards on the Central Coast, and left it to breathe a few minutes. Then she unpacked her bag, took off her travel clothes and wrapped a bath towel around herself. She poured a large glass of the wine and took it with her out to the hot tub.

The hot tub sat on the back deck, looking out over maybe twenty-five yards of nothing, to the top of a bluff that dropped twenty-five feet to rocks that met the Pacific. Francie loved sitting in the 99-degree warmth, regardless of the weather, and let her thoughts drain out into the ethers. Often, new ones came in to take their place. It was a very creative spot for her. A glass of wine enhanced the process. Between the sounds of the waves and the gentle throbbing of the bubbler, it was a perfect venue for relaxation and reflection.

While she would have chosen simply to keep her mind clear and just go with her senses, the mind, at least her mind, didn't usually operate on command. The tub helped her to purge the strain of the flight and to get back into the Pacific time zone. She might have watched the sun go down, but the fog was in, and the night fell without celebration.

The next morning, she was at her desk at six; she got up when the sun began to shine. She looked through the headlines on a half-dozen news sites online – she didn't bother with blogs, even those she might agree with – and she answered emails. Instead of waiting until a decent hour to call him back, she sent Franklin Hayes an email, suggesting that they meet and figure out what the campaign truly needed in terms of security.

An answer to her email arrived not minutes later. "Breakfast?"

"Sure," she wrote back, and then suggested "Bistro 211 at eight?" since it was close to his new campaign headquarters. She hadn't seen the place yet, and was interested to see what Ariane had had to deal with in terms of the technology and the layout.

"Sure," he wrote back. She liked that he wasn't the typical politician who took twenty words when one would do. She wondered if the public would appreciate how important that was, or simply think of him as different.

Francie left her house at 7:45, and when she arrived at the restaurant ten minutes later discovered that he was earlier. He was sitting in a chair at a table, leaving the banquette side for her to have her back against the wall. More points for him, she thought. He stood when she arrived, and when she had sat down, he excitedly showed her his new Pilot pen.

"You're right, it's great. Thank you for pointing it out."

"Sure," she said, repeating herself.

"I told the clerk that you had recommended the pen but wouldn't let me try yours. He gave me two to try. I chose the fine point."

"Life's little pleasures."

"Indeed." He was smiling broadly. Francie didn't know if it was because of her or the pen. They ordered quickly and then got down to business.

"Franklin," Francie opened with a smile.

"Yes, Francie," he responded similarly.

"I spent some time tracking down a line in one of the Nero Wolfe stories that I thought might be applicable to our situation. It was this: 'When a man hired an expert the only authority he kept was the right to fire.' Wolfe was rarely fired."

"I take your point," Hayes said humbly. "Politics is new to me, as is hiring a detective."

"Consulting detective," she corrected, maintaining a straight face.

"Consulting detective, of course," he corrected. "I'm fully prepared to allow you free rein. If I get something wrong, please let me know."

"I don't think it will come up," she told him, persuaded that he understood her.

"What's the next step?" he asked.

"After breakfast, I would like to take a look at your campaign office. Ariane is excellent at what she does. I like to see her work."

"She was very professional. She had everyone clear out for a long lunch so that she could do the work without questions or anyone being underfoot."

Francie nodded. "Then I want to write a memo to everyone concerned. You have four principal staffers and the memo will explain my duties, and invite them to contact me directly if they have any questions or issues about campaign security."

"Okay."

"It will also tell them that I am working quietly, not undercover, but not announced."

"That's right. Fine."

"When is the next time you'll have them all together? I could introduce myself and give them the memo."

"Saturday morning at ten at the campaign office."

"Would it work for me to be there then? I wouldn't have to stay for the whole meeting, if you don't want, but it would give me a chance to get a sense of your top people."

"Sure," he said again. "You are welcome to stay for the whole meeting. I'm hoping to keep it under two hours."

"Good. That should give me a feeling for who these people are."

After breakfast, the candidate and the consulting detective walked over to the campaign office. Francie did a survey of the offices, including sight lines through windows that might be vulnerable to snooping, and the wiring, both electric and telephones. She knew that Ariane would have all of these areas covered, but she wanted to be able to converse with her knowing what she was dealing with.

There were seven chairs in a circle in the middle of the campaign office when Francie arrived a few minutes before ten on Saturday morning. Promptly at the top of the hour, Franklin Hayes summoned everyone to the conference. At his direction she took the chair on his right. First came introductions, starting with her, since the others all knew each other. On her right was Sandy Horn, the communications director. About Francie's age, though about thirty pounds over-weight, she was also a refugee from television news in a couple of Midwest markets. To her right was Roger Toney, a good-looking thirty-something advance pro who had been working on mostly-Democratic campaigns since he was in his teens. Across the circle from Hayes was Beth Moriarty, Hayes's wife. An attractive woman, his age, formerly foxy. Francie had felt her looking at her but never caught her at it. To her right was Desmond Pritzer, a man in his sixties who looked tired, probably perennially; he was the treasurer. Next to the candidate was Brenda Poole, a young black woman, nondescript, early twenties, with a notebook in her lap. She was the candidate's personal assistant.

Hayes ran the meeting very smoothly, wasting no time, but making sure that everyone said what they needed to. Most of it was reporting on progress to date, anticipating a statewide launch in two months. It would be a challenging campaign, but with all that was going wrong in the country and the world, with the 78-year-old Feinstein polling below 50%, with the Republicans still to put up their own candidate, it was fair to call the situation fluid, at least.

Francie was impressed by the quality of the people Hayes had chosen. Many political newbies with money would simply go out and buy the highest-priced talent they could find. Hayes had found people who were probably more interested in his campaign than the money, though the salaries persuaded them that it wouldn't be a Quixotic affair. These people were serious, independent minds – except maybe the treasurer; but that position didn't require independence -- and the candidate had what it took to bring them together.

Their reporting was concise. No one was there to promote themselves, or for that matter, to earn strokes. Sandy Horn, the communications director, had considerable experience in polling ,and she spoke of plans to go into the field in another month to assess particular aspects of the Feinstein image and record. Roger Toney put a map of the state up on the wall to show where he would mount operations to pull in the liberal Republicans, the disappointed Democrats, and the independents who would be the key to the victory.

Pritzer, the treasurer, added a note of levity when he gave the bank balance and said, "We haven't spent a lot, which is good, because we haven't taken in anything. Except of course, from our honorable candidate. Thank you, Franklin."

The personal assistant was something of a surprise. She apparently was also the administrative person. She spoke of the need for weekly reporting, adding to the central contact lists, and staying current on their expense accounts with Desmond.

A lot was covered in the first hour, and then Hayes invited Francie to speak. First she told them of her background, both the broadcasting and the few political campaigns on which she had consulted. Then she handed out her introduction memo to the four assistants and to the candidate, telling his wife that she didn't know she was going to be attending, but that she was sure Hayes would share his with her. The memo was simple. It said that Francie would be consulting on security, to protect the campaign from any illegal intrusion, especially industrial spying. She also made it clear that she wanted to keep her participation in the campaign quiet; that's why there was no press release. If people knew about her working with the campaign, it would reduce her efficiency. "So please," she told them, "Keep this under your hats."

There were a couple of questions, but nothing complicated, and then Hayes closed with a few remarks about how exciting this all was; that they were going to make history. With that, they all stood up, and there was some milling about and Francie did some hand-shaking. Sandy, the other former broadcaster, had a number of industry war stories she was ready to share, and promised it would be another time, perhaps over a glass of something. Desmond gave Francie a 1099 to fill out. She told him she would bill as a corporation. Roger asked where she had lived in California and she told him, San Francisco briefly and now the Monterey Peninsula. And Brenda got all of her contact information.

Hayes had been huddling with his wife, but keeping an eye on everything. When he saw that Francie was free, he brought her over for a formal introduction. She was thoroughly gracious on the surface, but something about the candidate's wife caused Francie to be wary of the woman. She didn't know what it was, she didn't let it show, but it registered in the back of her mind, where Francie kept her alert messages.

Beth Moriarty was polite, but cool. Francie supposed that she was still smarting from her refusal to give her Hayes's security code number. She had to guess that he had found some way to explain to her why Francie was right, and while she accepted it, for the time being, she didn't buy it. Francie might have told her to just accept it, but that wouldn't have gone over too well, and Francie still wanted Hayes to win. More so, after seeing the people he had hired and the way he ran the meeting. She told herself, we need that kind of perspicacity and leadership in Washington so badly.

The others dispersed. It was Saturday and the campaign hadn't yet gotten seriously underway. These people had lives, she presumed; at least for a couple of months. Francie said her good-byes, and as she left, closing the door behind her, she noticed that Hayes and his wife were back in their huddle.

*   *   *   *   *

The following Wednesday Francie got a surprise, sort of, when she opened up *The Herald*. It used to be the *Monterey Peninsula Herald* but the then-owner a while back decided to spread out to Salinas and the further environs, obviously in an effort to drive up circulation, and consequently advertising revenues. But Salinas already had *The Californian* so oops, *The Herald* wound up jacking up their distribution and staffing costs, but not its revenues. When it had to cut back on expenses – surprise, surprise – it was the newsroom that got the cuts. Alas...

Anyway, the surprise was that there was an article about how Francie had been brought in as a consultant on the fledgling Hayes for Senate campaign. Okay, it wasn't a surprise. Franklin Hayes had brought her in explicitly because he was worried about security, and the article was proof that his fears were not unfounded. Francie couldn't say for sure that she knew who had leaked the information, not until the next day, when, as it happened, she was doing some food shopping.

Francie had long believed that if you're on the right track, the universe helps you along by putting people in your path. As in the I-was-just-thinking-about-you-syndrome. And, Oh, what a coincidence! Maybe. Anyway, she was in Trader Joe's when she ran into Milt Cassel, the reporter for *The Herald* who'd run the piece on her joining the Hayes campaign. He had written the piece without calling her, which she thought was less than professional. After all, they had met a few times at local events, and he knew that she had been a reporter herself. Maybe he had been on deadline, she thought, but didn't believe it.

He might have noticed her first but he pretended not to and turned and pushed his cart down another aisle. Francie circled around and when he made his turn at the end of the aisle, there she was.

"Hello, Milt," she said dryly.

"Oh, uh, hey, howzit goin'?"

"I need your help, Milt."

"Oh, me?"

"Yeah, you."

"What can I do to help you?"

"About that story about me working for Hayes," she began and watched him try to swallow.

"I can't talk about that. It was a source story," he said defensively.

"I'm not asking who the source was, Milt. I want your opinion on the motivation. Was it to hurt the campaign, or help? Surely you must have gotten a sense about what was behind this?"

"Yeah, oh, well, um, that's kind of privileged."

"Milt, I'm not asking for a fact but your opinion. What you thought? What was your impression? Surely you can share that with a fellow journalist."

He thought a minute. "Well, I think sh...I think maybe it was to hurt you, if you want the truth."

"Huh," Francie replied as if his false start didn't meaning anything to her. She kept her poker face on, but she knew that he had been going to say "she" after think. So to throw him off the track she said, "Hey, don't worry. I know who it was. I wouldn't have asked you if I didn't know she did it. That wouldn't have been professional."

He looked relieved, and Francie maintained the blasé look.

"Another question," she said, and the relief drained from his face. "Tell me, do you make a list when you shop?"

His face was such a blank you would have thought that he didn't have a thought in his head at that moment. "What?"

"When you shop, do you make a list?" Francie held up her list. "You know, write down what you don't want to forget?"

The wheels were turning and finally stopped when he couldn't imagine how she might be tricking him. "Um, sometimes. You know, if there are a lot of things."

"Right," she told him, as if it had been a test, and the relief returned. "Thanks, Milt," she said, and walked around him to continue her shopping, making sure to keep her expression flat until she got around the corner. Then she smiled and said to herself, "Bang-zoom."

*   *   *   *   *

What no one knew about the memos that Francie had passed around to Franklin Hayes and his four top aides at the meeting that Saturday was that they were all different; subtly but significantly. Each had a variation in spelling of one of the key words that she knew would be used in an article when the memo was leaked. There were also differences in the year she left broadcasting, for example, and in the call letters of the stations where she had worked. Plus a couple more tricks which she would use in later cases. So the moment she saw the article, she knew whose memo had been used.

She was not really surprised, but it complicated matters and she needed to figure things out before she acted. She had some time to think because the candidate was out of town on other business and wouldn't be back until the following Monday. There was no real urgency since the release of her affiliation with the campaign wasn't a big deal; she'd merely made it seem that way at the meeting. She would need a definite plan before he got back.

The quandary was how to do right by her client. Her sense was that he was going to have to quit the race. Yes, it was that big. There was a chance the situation could be salvaged, but she didn't see how. Then she got a call on Sunday from a fellow who was a manager at Trader Joe's. He knew her because a couple of years before, she'd spotted someone breaking into their store one night and had called the police in time to nab the thief.

So it was because he had seen the article in *The Herald* and learned that she was working on the campaign that he had called her now instead of the police. That was the first thing he told her when she answered the phone, and it certainly got her attention. He didn't want to talk about it on the phone, since there were too many people around, so she drove up to Monterey to meet with him.

When Francie arrived not fifteen minutes later, he walked outside with her. And then he dropped the bombshell. Beth Moriarty had left the store without paying for her groceries, worth over $200. A security guard had caught up with her in the parking lot, where first she denied it, and then she said she must have simply forgotten. Then she couldn't find her purse. She promised to come back with the money in an hour. It had been three hours. The manager was giving Francie the chance to keep the matter private.

She paid the bill immediately, and told him how grateful she was that he had called her. He said now they were even, which made it abundantly clear how unhappy he was with the situation. While he was not out any money, he'd gone out on a big limb by calling her first, and there could still be repercussions from the head office if he was found out. Francie promised him that nothing would be forthcoming from her end.

Of course it was Beth Moriarty, too, who had contacted *The Herald*. The coded memo that appeared in the paper was the one Francie had given to Hayes. She knew he wouldn't undermine his own campaign, and she wouldn't normally have thought that his wife would have, but she wouldn't she have been wrong.

It was one thing that she had revealed Francie's connection to the campaign. It was another that she was almost arrested for shoplifting. The fact that she had plenty of money made it obvious that she was suffering from significant mental issues. Whatever her reasons, she wanted to pull down the campaign, and there was no way that Franklin Hayes could stay in the race under those circumstances. If you don't have your wife's support, you won't have the voters'; at least not all you should expect, and probably need to win.

Francie called Hayes and asked him how he was getting home from the airport on the morrow. He told her he would probably take a cab.

"Why don't I give you a ride home?" she suggested.

There was a pause and he asked, "Did something come up?"

"Uh-huh."

"And you don't want to tell me about it now?"

"Not over the phone."

"That serious?"

"That serious."

She wasn't trying to be melodramatic. She was just answering his questions, honestly and in an even tone.

"Okay," he said, and confirmed the flight arrangements that he'd given to her previously.

"One more thing, Franklin. Don't tell your wife that I'll be picking you up. Say you're getting a lift from a colleague, or taking a cab."

Oh, lord," he said in a way that she inferred meant that he was aware that she was the source of the "that serious" problems.

"You'll be all right," she told him before signing off.

The next day Francie was at the Monterey terminal when his flight arrived. He had told her he didn't have stowed luggage, so they were out pretty quickly and into her car. Franklin Hayes was calm. He either had a sense of the problem and/or he had resigned himself to the magnitude of it. That would have meant he trusted her perspective, and she thought that was mighty perspicacious considering how long they had known each other. It said a lot about him, she knew.

As she turned onto Highway 68, heading toward the Highway One gate to Pebble Beach, she outlined the two situations that had arisen. He took it all quietly, not interrupting, not arguing. More points in his column. She felt him look over at her while she laid out the facts for him. He liked facts, even the ones he didn't like. When she had finished, he nodded and summed up the situation.

"You're right. I can't continue with this. For the campaign, or for my family."

"I'm sorry."

"I appreciate the way that you have handled this. I couldn't have asked for more or better."

"Yes, well..."

They rode in silence for several moments, both of them looking ahead. Then Francie said to him, "Franklin, why did you decide to run yourself? I mean, I like your ideas, as I told you, but you are different from all of the candidates I've met over the years."

He chuckled. "I never thought of myself as the candidate type. I'm not particularly patient with ignorance, and not very social. But I knew my ideas were right. I looked around to find someone to run with them but I came up empty. I decided that considering how limited most of the candidates I had seen were, I could – I would have to – take the role myself. It wasn't my first choice."

"What about your wife? Was she supportive of your plan?"

He was quiet for a moment. "Beth has some problems. She was taking medication for them, but I think the stress of the campaign – just the thought of it – pushed her over the edge." He looked at Francie, and then added, "I think she also found you a threat."

She looked at him quickly; she didn't like to take her eyes off the road. "What kind of threat? Personal?"

"Yes," he said, "but not necessarily amorous. She could read me, my energy, that I found you very attractive. It was more that I was excited about who you were, and that you would be part of the campaign. I would never be unfaithful to her, which was something I know she knew earlier, but her thinking hasn't been so clear lately."

"I am so sorry, Franklin. I guess I didn't get the job done for you the way you wanted. I may have precipitated this."

"No, no, Francie. This wasn't you. If anyone, it was my fault for not seeing the situation with Beth for what it was. Her demons took over. I don't know that there was anything anyone could have done about it."

Francie pulled into the circular driveway in front of his modest – for Pebble Beach – mansion. She felt him stiffen suddenly and she looked over to see his wife coming out of the front door.

"Stop here," he ordered sharply but not loudly and she did. "Stay in the car," he told her without looking at her. He jumped out of the car, and walked toward his wife. His window had been open, and while she could hear him talking to her, Francie couldn't hear what he was saying. As he approached her, he opened his arms wide and she moved into them. One arm around him, the other by her side.

That's when Francie saw the gun in her hand. But it was pointed at the ground. She watched as they held each other, and then watched as his hand slide down her side until he had covered hers. Then he had the gun. He turned her and they walked back into the house together, leaving the door open.

Francie took his bag from the back seat and carried it carefully to the front door. She put it down quietly on the front stoop, turned and seconds later was driving back toward the Highway One gate.

*   *   *   *   *

Franklin Hayes phoned Francie the next morning. He thanked her for the way she handled everything. She returned the compliment.

"I told Beth that I had decided I wasn't a politician and that I shouldn't be a candidate. She agreed. I told her that she had nothing to worry about. Then she fell asleep in my arms."

"I think you will probably always be happy with the decision. The people in politics these days, even or especially in Congress, have an unfortunate talent of being able to lie to your face, and those are your allies. Monterey is much nicer."

There was wistfulness in his voice. "I really thought that I could make a difference. Not me the person, the candidate, but I thought my platform would resonate with enough people that I could win, and actually shift the thinking in Congress. Was that silly of me?"

"Maybe," she allowed, "but most of the people on Capitol Hill have been, as you noted yourself, compromised by the special interests money. I think you would have found it terribly frustrating."

That didn't mollify him much. He already knew that. "But we have to do something, Francie. We know what's wrong, we know how to fix it. We can't just wallow in our cynicism."

"I don't think it's cynicism. I think it's reality. Sometimes you have to let Nature take its course. Martyrdom isn't an attractive road. Think in terms of surfing. You have to wait for the wave."

"I can't argue with your logic, but I would like to be sure that I don't sit out any longer than I should. I don't want to waste what I know.

Francie was quiet for a moment and then offered him a new route. "What if you could wage a campaign without being the candidate? What if you could create the kind of sea change in politics that you are about? And you could do it from here. You wouldn't have to leave your family."

"What? You're the tooth fairy?"

She laughed. "I know it sounds pie-in-the-sky, but a friend of mine has sketched out what he calls the 28th amendment. It is a constitutional amendment that would reform our elections process, by taking the money out of the process, shortening the election season, keeping political ads off television, and radio, and generally cleaning up the system."

"That sounds wonderful," he said. There was a new lilt in his voice."But how would you get something like that through Congress. You'd need two-thirds vote, and I can't imagine that a fraction of them would vote to cut off the advantage of their incumbency."

"Of course you're right about that, but there is the alternative of going through the states. It would mean getting 38 state legislatures to approve the amendment."

"Oh my goodness," said the erstwhile candidate excitedly, "That would be possible, wouldn't it, in today's political climate? So many people are upset. This would give them the opportunity to focus their anger on Congress."

"With their approval rating below ten percent, exactly."

"Very interesting," he said, and Francie could hear his brain working. "What's the status of the amendment? Where is it? Who's your friend?"

"He's a retired journalist who's turned to writing novels because he decided he was just banging his head against the wall with the facts. He emailed me that two years ago the financial industry spent $1.3 billion dollars through more than 2,500 lobbyists to fight reform. That came to more than $2 million for every member of Congress."

"Banging his head against the wall. That sounds familiar."

"He lives in Monterey, and what he's done is define the changes that need to be made. It's not in legal terms, but we know a fellow down south who is one of the country's foremost constitutional scholars. He would know how to put the wording right."

"Francie, this is fascinating. Plus I've already got a campaign team, and a headquarters. This really could be the way to make change, the kind of change and to the degree that we need to get our country back on track. Take the power away from the corporate campaign investors, and we could get some serious people in Congress and the White House. When can

I meet your friend?"

"I'll arrange it," she told him. And she did.

The Francie LeVillard Mysteries

Raggedy Ann

Francie LeVillard was one of those people – rare among women, especially – who never wanted children. Her own, or for that matter, anyone else's. She was good with them when she had to be, but she only remained in the presence of them when they were very well behaved. Being single, and not a mom, had enabled her to follow her professional interests without other responsibilities. Interests such as working as a television news reporter for stations in Washington, D.C., and New York City. And for the last ten years as a consulting detective, work that often meant flirting with danger. Though let it be quickly noted that she didn't court it, but when she did, overcoming it was her only.

The great-granddaughter of François LeVillard, an eminent detective with the Deuxième Bureau in Paris who had worked with Sherlock Holmes, Francie not only had the requisite genes to become a world-class investigator, she loved justice as much as she did journalism. Whether she was shackling terrorists smuggling nuclear triggers into the United States, or plugging a leak in a noble political campaign, Francie wanted comeuppance for the evil-doers. As a friend put it, she was "attractive, bright and bad news for bad guys."

So you have a picture in your mind of this significant person, Francie is attractive, but not glamourous. She was always more comfortable being seen for her intellect and humor than just being pretty. Five-seven and 135 pounds, she had dark hair not long enough to get in her eyes which framed a slightly oval face of tawny skin color. Mostly she dressed for comfort, which meant jeans, a loose-fitting shirt, and a jacket that extended over her hips; and often to hide a pistol on her belt.

This case did not require a gun. In fact, there wasn't even a client, just the need for resolution; for the truth, Francie was relentless. It started with a discovery that she read about in a news item online. Bones were discovered fifty yards off a secondary trail at Point Lobos. This is a marvelous state park south of Carmel on the California Central Coast whose wonderful acreage was donated by a number of private owners. It's a very spiritual place, highlighted by delicious flora and surrounded by a rugged shoreline and crashing waves. Whoever chose to bury the body there did so with love.

The bones had been found by a pair of aged flower hunters from San Jose who had gingerly plied their way through the trees and gorse and beheld a scapula sticking out of the dirt. The woman was a retired pediatrician or else she might not have realized what she was seeing. She also had the sense not to approach it once she saw what it was. She stood looking down at what she could only guess, dispatching her husband to notify a park ranger. Her husband had done so, returning with the ranger who lacked the sense to have called the sheriff. The once-doctor needed to exert her own practiced authority to keep him away from the site and to get him to call the real authorities. Begrudgingly, he relented and a sheriff's deputy was summoned.

The first bit of identification was supplied by the county forensic pathologist, an aikido pal of Francie's named Lolly Perlis. She said that they were old. The bones, that is; not the person whose bones they had been before she didn't need them anymore. Over coffee late one early June morning, after their workout, Lolly told Francie what she had learned from a cursory examination of the boxful of human remains that had been brought to her lab.

"Someone else might not have known what it was," Lolly said. "Children's bones don't look very different to someone who doesn't know better. Especially when they've been in the ground so long." She took a sip of her coffee. "I wish I had time to really examine them, but they're too old."

She saw the quizzical look on Francie's face.

"There is too much work," she declared, her tone bent by her anguish. "Current cases, new cases....they need to be assessed for prosecution. The DA wants to file charges, so I have to give them the evidence. These bones are maybe 60 years old. We're talkin' a child buried some time around the Korean War, for goodness sakes. They're not gonna crack that case."

"Ever?" Francie asked.

"Oh, bah! Sure, when I get the two assistants I've been pleading for, and then after the gangs finish killing themselves off we might catch up."

"This one has gotten to you, hasn't it, Lolly?" Francie asked softly.

The doctor nodded her head affirmatively, for a long time, until her eyes were moist and she had to sniff and clear her throat. "It was a child, Francie. Children aren't supposed to die."

"How old?"

"Maybe three. Hard to tell." She peered at me. "I think it was a girl. It's difficult to tell when they're so young, you know? It's not until they approached adolescence that their young bodies indicate where they are going, at least the skeletal address. But I have a feeling that it was a little girl. Kinda strong feeling, but I don't know why. So sad."

"Any cause of death?" Francie asked.

Lolly shook her head. "Not from a cursory look. No broken bones," she seemed pleased to report. "No sign of violence."

"Considering where they found her, maybe it was illness. I guess that would be better," Francie thought aloud.

Lolly agreed and then shook her head and then smiled. "I think she was buried with love. I think she had a doll with her. They brought back two buttons which might have been the eyes on a Raggedy Ann doll. My mother had one like that. That's what made me think it was. Square black plastic eyes."

"Would you like me to see if I can turn up anything on this?"

"Oh, Francie that would be great if you could," her friend said, effusive in her surprise and gratitude. "I'll take another look at her when I get back – that stupid drug dealer can wait – and I'll let you know what I can find. Maybe get closer on the age, and get something on her height and weight."

After she left Lolly, in much better spirits, Francie drove around Monterey on errands, and in the course of her ambling managed to track down Ted Boros on her cellphone. A deputy sheriff, Boros was one of the sharper knives in the department's drawer. She knew that not only from his reputation, but from her own experience working with him.

Boros had been attracted to police work for the right reasons. Not the gun, uniform, and authority, but because he had a natural aptitude for understanding people, many who didn't understand themselves. He once told her that he might have become a psychiatrist, but he knew he would never have made it through medical school.

Francie told him about her chat with Lolly who was also one of his favorite colleagues. They were great puzzle solvers, though they went about their work with very different pieces before them. Lolly wasn't a people person, at least not live ones. Boros enjoyed people, even the black hats and the crazies.

"What can you tell me about what you found?"

"Not much more than what Lolly told you."

"Okay, I'll take less than much. Whaddya got?"

He told her that the body had been buried with care. They could tell that from the alignment of the bones. He thought Lolly was right about the doll. "From where we found the buttons, the doll, if that's what it was, could have been in her arms."

"Umf, that makes it more human, doesn't it?"

"This one's got to you too?"

"Maybe a little. What else?"

"That's about it, except that she was buried deep, probably three feet, which is a lot. Whoever did the digging didn't want some animal to dig it up. The rains we had this spring were heavy, and probably some road work re-channeled the drainage, causing the earth above to erode. Plus it's been years out there." He paused and then added. "I guess it was her time."

*　　*　　*　　*　　*

Attracted to the uniform and gun and authority for the wrong reasons were people like Zina Postelle. A large, unattractive woman who should have checked with a plastic surgeon to see if her constant sneer might be fixed, she was immune to courtesy and humor. Francie knew that from personal experience as she had run into her a couple of times on the path between Monastery Beach and the mouth of the Carmel River. Each time, if she was jogging or just walking, Francie would offer her a smile or a brief wave but there was no response from the ranger. It was as if the woman were too busy to acknowledge a fellow human being, as she was looking out for terrorists or some other threat in one of the most idyllic settings on the planet.

Oh well...and then there was the occasion when the ranger did pay attention to her. Francie was walking that day, enjoying the beneficial sunshine rays – unusual for June on the Central Coast – and dictating notes for a novel she was writing into a digital tape recorder in the outside pocket of her light jacket. Francie didn't need great quality sound; she just needed to be able to transcribe her notes when she got home. Absorbed in her "writing," Francie wasn't paying serious attention to her surroundings.

She did notice a dog trotting toward her from the direction of the river, and she stopped for him, or her. It was a Shepherd-something mix with a friendly face and wagging tail, and she rubbed its head. Then she continued on her way. She hadn't gone ten paces when she heard what sounded like a herd of elephants – okay, one elephant – coming up behind her. She naturally moved over to the right side of the path to let the herd go by but it didn't go by. It stopped.

"Hey," said the large woman in a ranger uniform with a red – from running – face. "You know that you have to keep dogs on a leash."

"I guess so," Francie said. Not having a dog, she didn't know for sure but she had heard that from people who had their dogs on leashes. (The rule disappointed both the people and the dogs, and wasn't a rule on the lovely Carmel-by-the-Sea beach or the miles of Pebble Beach shorelines.) The ranger seemed to take some satisfaction in Francie's, um, admission, and said, "Then I guess you don't get a warning, do you?"

"What do I need to be warned about?" Francie asked, suddenly alert.

The ranger looked down at the dog whom she'd stopped to pet when it came up to her.

"I don't think he's dangerous," Francie told her.

"That's not the point and you know it," Ranger Postelle declared officiously as she took out her ticket book. "I'd like to see some identification, please."

The please was not said in a way to evoke any thought of grace.

"For what?"

"Because I told you to, that's for what."

"Are you writing me a ticket?"

"That's right, sister, for breaking the law."

"What law? I didn't break any law. This isn't..."

She stopped writing and looked at her hard.

"Name?"

"You're making a mistake."

The ranger's face turned a harsher shade of red and she demanded, "Name?"

Francie knew this wasn't going to be settled on the spot, which was fine with her. The ranger was wearing a leather belt that had on it a baton, a can of mace, handcuffs, and a large gun. Francie didn't want any of those items to be in the ranger's hands. So she gave her all of the information that she asked for. When they were done, the ranger looked around and asked, "Where's the dog?"

"I don't know. I was here with you."

The ranger didn't think that was funny. She ripped the ticket out of her book with extra force and handed Francie a copy. "You can pay the fine or contest this arrest in court."

"Will you be there..." – Francie looked on the ticket for the woman's name – "Is it Miss Postal?" she asked, putting her own spin on the pronunciation.

"I am California State Park Ranger Zina Postelle," she declared, "and yes, I will be there."

"See ya," Francie said with a mindless smile and walked on, proud that her normal lack of patience with officious authorities hadn't turned into an incident.

* * * * *

"It's amazing, truly amazing!" said Lolly Perlis. She hadn't even waited for Francie to say hello; she just gave her time to get the phone to her head.

"Good morning, Lolly," Francie managed. Lolly was one of the few people who called late and Francie didn't mind, so much.

"Not yet, Francie. Still an hour to midnight. Were you

in bed already? I forgot that you aren't a night owl. Sorry, but I had to call anyway." Then she appended in something of a scold, "You're sleeping your life away, girl!"

"Is that why you called me?" Francie chuckled.

"No, I would never tell you how to live your life."

She didn't point out that she had just done so. Instead Francie told her, "Always good to hear your voice, Lolly," as she rose to the next stage of wakefulness.

"Francie, I was looking at those bones and you'll never guess what I discovered."

Francie was awake enough to know that she had to turn on the light and reach for an ever-present pad and pen. "What?"

"Well, they never would have been able to do this sixty years ago, of course, not even ten, but we have this new chromatograph that is as close to magic as science can get."

"I'm pleased for you, Lolly. What did you find out?"

"We can tell the age of the person at death, and when they died, plus their sex, though sometimes it can still be confusing when they're under five or six. But anyway, this girl was forty months – I told you it was a girl – and she was from Central Michigan. I can't get it closer than that. But also, and this should help, the dolls eyes, they were only used in 1951, just that one year."

Francie was hurriedly writing notes as she asked, "Anything on the parents?"

"Hey, aren't you supposed to say great and wonderful and stuff?"

"And stuff," Francie replied. "I'm much better when I'm awake, Lol, and I can read my script. You did great, now could you pull up anything on the parents?"

"Mother was Scandinavian, probably Finnish, and the father was UK, probably Welsh."

Francie laughed and said, "You are incredible, Lolly, you and your magic machine."

"Aw shucks, you're just saying that," the scientist demurred, but then with her enthusiasm somehow immediately restored she asked, "So how can you sleep now?"

Francie laughed. "I probably can't, now, thanks to you."

"You're welcome. I won't call again until tomorrow, if I find something else."

"You're a pal," Francie told her and clicked off. She put her pad and pen back on the bedside table and turned off the light. She re-entwined herself around her pillow and told herself to go back to sleep. Herself wasn't listening. If experience was any guide, she knew that trying to get back to sleep rarely worked. After a few minutes, she gave up the ghost, so to speak, and, wide awake, got up to do her homework. Something about using too much energy in the trying would keep her brain active, and hence, "Hello, I'm awake for a while."

Wrapped in her thick terrycloth bathrobe, she booted

up her computer and then went to the kitchen to start some water for tea. She returned to her office and waited the final long seconds for the computer to await her nimble touch. (For those of you for whom this is important, Francie uses PCs. She has since she was a teen. She was never interested in Apples because she liked to be able to go behind the curtain, if need be, to get the machine to do what she wanted. She wasn't a techie by any means, but she had gotten to a level where she rarely had to call one.)

First thing was to check her email, and the most recent was from Lolly, apologizing for waking her and telling her to get on with her research. She was indeed a dear person, and committed to getting things righted when they were wrong. In her work, often things were wrong because there were no obvious answers. She often supplied them by applying her marvelous mind to whatever puzzle came before her. And like Francie, her favorite cases were those that not only required the use of those "leetle grey cells" as Hercule Poirot called them, but those situations that would, as she said, benefit the common weal. No wonder they were friends in addition to colleagues.

Next, Francie checked the world, national and state/local headlines. This was her normal wake-up routine in the morning, and since she'd been awakened, well, it must be morning, and so to her routine. As it turned out, there was little in the way of developments that warranted reading past the headlines since she'd shut down the computer two hours earlier. And then the kettle whistled for her.

A few minutes later, settled in her office with her

jasmine tea, she started pouring through state and local police records in the Wolverine State. The Internet is a marvelous place for research, of course, but more for modern records of this type than older ones. Limited resources meant that cold cases, and certainly ancient ones in terms of police investigations, were not a priority, especially when it came to entering the data into online files. That was changing, slowly, as companies and universities applied their new technologies and their personnel pools to digitizing further into the past.

Francie was arbitrarily figuring that this girl was born around mid-century, give or take a couple of years. She was certainly ready to change the parameters, but that was her starting point. She didn't know what she was looking for, that is, whether the child's death was the result of a criminal act, so she first searched for open or closed criminal cases involving children from Michigan, ages two to five, white female, which narrowed things down considerably.

Amazing, that's what Lolly had said first thing to her, and amazing it was when she looked at the results on the screen. There were two cases, and instantly Francie knew she had found the little girl. Both girls – white, aged three – had been reported missing, presumed abducted in 1952 in central Michigan; in all of Michigan for that matter. There had been no such cases the year before or the year after. In one case, the girl had been on the radar of the local social services agency because the other child in the family had been reported by a teacher for bruises. The suspicion was that the girl in question had probably been the victim of similar treatment and had not survived, and that the parents had disposed of her somewhere.

The girl Francie was seeking had not been ill-treated. No broken bones, and buried with love. Francie was sure that she was the other case. How did she know? She would explain it this way: Our intuitive sense – our sixth sense – is both the most powerful and the least credited. Detective work, like journalistic investigation, is most often successful when based on intuition; except in the most obvious cases when it isn't needed. But even in those cases, one knows, inside, whether what the evidence or research tells you is correct.

Francie's male colleagues over the years would tease her, complaining that women had a natural intuitive sense that they themselves lacked. "Nonsense," she would tell them, seriously upbraiding those whom she thought were just lazy. "Men have the same power; they just don't use it because they never had to rely on it as women did, just to survive."

*   *   *   *   *

Marla Ellen Duff was three years old when she was reported snatched out of her rocking chair on the front porch of her parents' home in a middle class neighborhood in Brighton, about 35 miles west northwest of Detroit. This was significant because the girl's father, Marion Albert Duff, was an airline pilot for Northwest Orient, and he flew a DC-6 to Seattle and San Francisco.

Without having any idea why the girl had been

reported missing, Francie knew in her gut that it was a tragic story. She also knew that it had been personal rather than criminal. Deeper searching turned up the mother, Marja Jussila Duff, who had been institutionalized shortly after the disappearance and had died two years later. Duff, the husband and father, had stayed with NWO but had shifted his base to San Francisco, flying western routes to Tokyo and Seoul, moving up to jet aircraft and finally retiring at the mandatory age of sixty in 1983, at which time he had moved to...Monterey.

One of Francie's distant mentors was Rex Stout. His Nero Wolfe character couldn't have been farther from her than she could imagine. He weighed a seventh of a ton, lived in a brownstone on 35th street in Manhattan, and almost never went out. While he had one of the most remarkable minds in the history of detection, it was acutely deliberate; intuition never came into play. But that didn't mean that he wasn't vitally important to those who followed, and indeed Francie found him immensely quotable.

She remembered one of his most prescient observations when she found the information about Duff. It was what Wolfe had said about coincidence: "In a world that operates largely at random, coincidences are to be expected, but any one of them must always be mistrusted."

Francie didn't have a doubt in her mind that some misfortune had befallen the Duffs, and that the father had buried the daughter at Point Lobos sixty years earlier. Her gut also told her that if he were still alive, Duff would be living nearby. She went back to bed and was soon asleep.

*   *   *   *   *

The next morning Francie called Lolly, sounding as cheery as she could. "I think I found her."

"What?" she all but screamed her delight. "Already? How did you do that?"

Francie's cheery tone segued back into her normal subdued voice. "A friend called me in the middle of the night and I couldn't get back to sleep." No comment. "So I got up and on my version of the magic machine – that's knowing how to search the Internet – I came up with what I think is the family."

"Get out! Tell me more."

"No, not yet. I have a little more tracking down to do."

"And you called why?"

"You sound like the Jewish mother I never had, thank goodness."

"And?"

"I called you because you should know that you're not the only one who works at all hours."

"I don't work at all hours," she protested.

"Uh-huh, you expect me to believe that you leave your work at the office, Lolly? Puh-leeze."

"But I don't bring my work home, not all the way home. I leave it in my car and I work on it when I'm driving to and from the office."

"Oh, well that makes all the difference. Pardon my faux affront."

"You're forgiven, but why won't you tell me what you found out already?"

"'Cause I don't want you to go off half-cocked."

"You know I wouldn't," Lolly said, sounding hurt.

But Francie had heard the sound before, and she didn't let it get to her, again. "And I called because I wanted to know if there was anything else about the girl that you either knew for sure or maybe guessed."

"Hmm." She made that humming sound for her deliberately, and Francie appreciated it because it meant Lolly was thinking. It was like watching the hourglass cursor on the computer screen showing that it was working.

"I can't give you anything else except maybe that I don't think she was breast-fed."

Francie was floored. "You can tell that, or is that a guess?"

"Somewhere in between," Lolly responded simply. "I haven't written it in a paper, but I'm pretty sure you can tell by the bone composition how much of it was from her own source, and how much of it wasn't. She was a lot of wasn't."

"Lolly, you are amazing. Not just your machine, but you. I'll call you when I know something."

"Francie...?" her voice softer and very personal.

"Yes, Lolly?"

"One more thing. I can't remember seeing bones with so few abrasions or breaks or any damage at all. She was taken very good care of."

"Yeah, it felt like that, didn't it? It didn't feel like a crime."

"She appreciates what you're doing, Francie."

Francie had to take in and let out a deep breath to give herself the moment to unlock the emotional constriction in her throat. "Hey, you started this, Lolly, and flights of angels sing thee to thy rest."

Her friend laughed lightly and said, "Sounds nice, but tell them I'm not ready yet." Then she paused and in a moment added quietly, "Not like this little girl. I think she was ready."

*   *   *   *   *

Cap'n Al, as he was referred to at the Monterey Gardens Center for Senior Living, had joined the airlines two weeks after he was released from the military. He'd flown two dozen bombing attacks over Europe, and had come home unscathed. He had married his high school sweetheart, and three years later they'd had a child. Later the child had disappeared. That's what the people at the senior center had been told, and in a voice that had told them not to press further on the subject. It certainly wasn't the first time that generations had been irretrievably cleaved, and knowing Cap'n Al as a warm and generous human being, the thought of miscreant behavior never entered a single mind. They lived in different worlds.

Al Duff was in fairly good shape for a man who had celebrated his 88th birthday two days before Christmas. He was trim, he had his mental faculties, and he seemed to be one of the few inmates, so to speak, who wasn't wondering why he was still alive. That was what Francie learned from Danielle Arnoff, the executive director of The Gardens, as it was called. She was giving Francie the unvarnished version because their paths had crossed a few years earlier, and the Danni knew she could trust Francie implicitly.

They were standing on the veranda, looking out at a broad lawn dotted with chaise lounges, many of them occupied by people who had wrapped themselves in blankets against the cool of The Peninsula summer. "That's Cap'n Al, over there," she said, nodding her head slightly in the direction of a distinguished-looking fellow in grey slacks and heavy blue sweater standing next to a woman sitting in a horse-blanket cocoon. "He's a favorite here, both of the staff because he never asks for anything, and the residents who seem to get a rise out of speaking with him. Maybe because he refuses to discuss physical ailments, which is all almost everyone else wants to talk about."

Francie couldn't be sure but she thought he knew that Danni was speaking about him, even though it didn't seem that he was looking in their direction. In a few moments he appeared to finish his conversation with the woman. He walked over to a koi pond and stood looking at its inmates. Francie left the director to her myriad tasks and walked slowly across the lawn to introduce herself to Al Duff. He was probably just under six feet, and she imagined that he'd dropped his weight over the years, to what looked like 180 pounds. Trim, but by no means gaunt.

He didn't turn around to face her until Francie was ten feet away. He couldn't have heard her coming since she was walking on grass and not making any noise. It might have been a sense of timing, or that he saw a reflection somewhere. He wasn't surprised to see her. Two steps later she stopped and gave him a chance to take her in. He focused his bright blue eyes laser-like on her face and said calmly, maybe with the slightest quaver in his voice, "You found her."

*   *   *   *   *

Francie might have been surprised, but she wasn't. She nodded, and watched the color suddenly drain from his face. She slipped up next to him and helped him sit on the broad stone shelf that rimmed the pond, sitting down beside him as he did so, her arm around him to make sure that he wouldn't fall. "Do you need something? Should I get a nurse?"

He shook his head, and then let it hang forward. In a minute, he slowly raised himself and she could see that he had regained most of his color. "It's funny," he said as if to no one at all, "but I've been waiting for this moment for so long, and when it finally came, I was surprised."

"Would you like some coffee, or something stronger perhaps? Some brandy? Do they serve alcohol here?" she asked.

He laughed. "Of course they serve alcohol here. The place would be empty if they didn't." He patted her gently on her knee. "No, really, I'm all right." Then in a stronger voice he said, "My apologies," he told her, looking at her again. "Where are my manners? Perhaps you would like something," and he started to rise.

Her arm around him held him down. "I'm fine, thank you, Mr. Duff. It is Mr. Duff, isn't it?"

He chuckled, "It would be one helluva story if it weren't."

"That it would," she agreed, smiling. "My name is Francie LeVillard."

His gaze at her narrowed. "The consulting detective?" he asked, and she nodded. "I think I read something about you. The modern Sherlock Holmes, it said. Is that how you found me?"

"I think we have some considerable conversing in front of us, Mr. Duff," Francie began.

"Please, not Mr. Duff. Al, or what they call me around here, Captain Al – Cap'n Al – if you must."

"I'll start with Cap'n Al then. Where might you be most comfortable? Should I take you out to lunch?"

A smile brightened on his face. "That would be a nice treat," he told her.

"What do you like to eat?"

"Everything that they don't serve here."

Francie laughed.

"No, actually, the food here is quite good. It's just...unimaginative. They can't attract anyone good to cook for people most of whom are on controlled diets."

She shrugged, "Makes sense, I suppose." They stood up together, but she kept her arm around him to make sure that he was all right. He seemed fine. "Do you need to check out or anything?"

"As a matter of fact I don't have to, but I make it a practice to. Or did. When I would leave. I don't think I've been off these grounds in five years. Not since I gave up my driver's license. I went through a stop sign. Didn't hit anything or hurt anyone, but it was a warning and I heeded it. This will be a treat."

They walked back together in the direction of the main building, and as they approached, Danni Arnoff appeared. "Danni," Al said, "I told you I was still a catch. This cute young thang has insisted on taking me out to lunch."

"I don't know if your reputation can take another boost, Captain Duff."

They all laughed, and Al and Francie headed toward the parking lot. She wasn't sure if he didn't feel a little more frail to her than the man she had first seen. She didn't have her arm around him or feel a need to monitor his step, but it felt as though he hadn't fully recovered from the shock of learning why she was there.

She opened the passenger door of her car for him, closing it again when he was firmly ensconced. He had his belt on before she was around the other side of the car. Pilots know the importance of being buckled in. She got in and buckled up and started them in the direction of the other world. "So where would you like to eat, Al? Or what? My treat."

He gave her a sweet smile, but behind it was a sea of thoughts that had threatened to engulf him; decades of fears, painful memories, and no doubt, guilt. When you have that long to think, and no one to talk to but yourself, myriad determinations are made and overturned, and confusion often reigns. Time does not heal all wounds. The last thing that might be clear to him was what he might want to eat, so she made the decision for them.

"How about the Fishwife, over in Pacific Grove? They have fresh seafood, and other things if you'd prefer."

He just turned to look out the front window and nodded his head in approval. She swung the car out in the direction of Highway One, climbed toward the top of Carmel Hill and turned off onto Route 68, climbing again past the hospital and then back down the ridge toward the ocean. It was 11:30 when they arrived at the restaurant, so she was able to park right in front.

As they walked in, they were greeted warmly by the colorful Anita, a lunchtime fixture at the Fishwife, who seated them at the premier table in a front corner. It gave them a view of the ocean several hundred yards away, sitting under the marine layer. Al declined an alcoholic libation, opting instead for an Arnold Palmer and Francie joined him. She looked at him over the top of her menu, watching him take great pleasure in looking over the offerings. He looked up and saw her watching him.

"You know, it might not be such a good thing that you said you were treating," he cautioned me.

"Why is that?" she asked.

"I might have an appetizer and dessert, too," he answered, his eyes twinkling.

"Uh-oh," she responded. "I never would have thought a man in your condition would eat so much. Huh. Well, a promise is a promise."

He looked at Francie, or at least in her direction, but he was seeing something – someone – much further away, in miles and times, who produced tears in his eyes. He pulled out a handkerchief, wiped his eyes, sniffed, and blew his nose. "How curious," he told her, "that after all of these years – decades – of waiting for this day, and I'm not ready for it."

"I don't know why you are saying that," she told him gently. "How would you expect you should react? That's a long time waiting for something so important."

He sniffed again and, persuaded that he wouldn't need it again, he put away his handkerchief. "Please, tell me everything. Did you find her?"

She shook my head. "A friend of mine, and a colleague, Lolly Perlis, is a forensic examiner. Someone had come across the remains and they were delivered to her. She is a very dear woman, and she was moved by what she found, that it was a little girl. She told me and I was touched by what she had discovered. The new science enabled her to pinpoint where the child was from, and I did some investigating online. Your situation was the one that fit. Plus I had a feeling it had to be you."

Sensing that he wasn't quite ready to explain, Francie took her time going through the scientific detail, in particular the origins of his wife and himself. That brought a smile to his face. "Yes, her parents had emigrated from Helsinki, and mine were from Liverpool, both after the Great War, as it was called then. They found work on the assembly lines in Detroit."

By this time their first course had been delivered. Al had ordered clam chowder and Francie a salad. He ate slowly, savoring every bite in a way she'd rarely seen someone do before. He had finished only half of the cup of soup when the main courses arrived. The waitress asked if he was finished with his chowder, but he said "no" and pushed it off to the side of the table. He sat looking over his seafood platter with excitement on his face. He looked across the table at her sea bass and she could tell from his expression that he knew he had made the better choice.

For several minutes they ate in silence and then he asked her in a clear, strong voice, but without any charge on it, "Why did you look for me?"

"I thought you would be wanting completion. That you were waiting for it."

It clearly wasn't the answer he expected, but it satisfied him. "That's true, you know. I hadn't thought about it that way. I think at the beginning, I just thought someone would find her, and then they would find me, somehow, and maybe I would be arrested or something. I didn't know. There was so much time to think, and I could never get her out of my mind. She was an angel. Truly an angel."

He might have been moved to tears, but he wasn't. Perhaps he had cried himself out already, if that ever happens, or, more likely, he was allowing a sense of release to provide him with the relief he had so long needed, even if he weren't conscious of that need.

"Al, I don't think there's anything to worry about. Even not knowing the details of what happened, I can all but assure you that you are not in any kind of jeopardy."

He looked at her, thoughtfully and long. "No, I didn't do anything wrong, except report a lie to the police, hide a body, and then bury it in another state." There was a tinge of bitterness in his voice, but it was mostly old anger. He turned his attention back to his lunch for several minutes. "I think you have a right to know what happened."

Francie held up both palms toward him gently, and said, "I don't need to know anything. Tell me only if you want me to know."

"And you will tell your friend, yes?"

She gave him a wry smile. "If that's all right with you. I don't have to, but she has a strong connection to your daughter. She's why I am here with you now."

He nodded his head slowly in agreement. "It won't matter soon, but you have my blessing to tell her. You're right. She brought this about. She may not have found my dear Marla, but she helped you to find out who she was, and to find me. Yes. You may tell her, and please, Miss LeVillard, express to her my gratitude."

*   *   *   *   *

There was a fleeting thought to invite him to call her Francie, but it wasn't the time. Nor would it be for the next half-hour as he recounted the events that had brought them together more than sixty years later. His story was not really a surprise. She didn't know the details before, but she had had a sense of the drama.

It had been a tough birth – the labor lasted most of 22 hours – and a nurse who was in it for the duration wasn't sure that the baby had come through unscathed. But in the late Forties, there wasn't the technology that might have caught something, or not, and all folks back then could do was hope for the best.

It turned out that wasn't enough. Worse, all the doctors could say was that this remarkably angelic child was not developing normally. Her physical body was slightly smaller than was expected, but more extraordinary was that she never made a sound. No gurgling, no words, and most alarming, ironically, was that she never cried. They had never before seen an infant who didn't cry.

They did some tests when she was about a year old, but all they managed to do was take the smile off the child's face. It wasn't after but a couple of visits that the mother refused to take her to the doctors any more, and after that the smile was always present, even as she slept.

So for the next two years, Al felt both his daughter and his wife leaving him. The baby in a failing body, and the woman with a mind that couldn't cope.

"She was such a dear little girl, a true angel." He sniffed, and gave a half laugh. "She was such a good girl. I think somehow she knew that she was here for just a short time and would enjoy it. I think my wife knew, too, but couldn't deal with it. It tore her apart at the end. That's why I did what I did."

The little girl just didn't grow; her condition didn't change. But her mother went downhill during the last two years. By the time the child died, the woman was on the verge of hysteria. Al continued to fly because he couldn't stand to be home where there was nothing to do but watch his wife come further apart.

Then one morning he returned after a trip across the Pacific. As he climbed out of his car, he was surprised to see the tiny rocking chair he'd made for Marla sitting on the porch of their home empty. Marla spent every day in that chair when the weather was favorable. In the summer, she might be there in a light dress, while in the cooler months of spring and fall she might be snuggled in a playsuit. This was late May, and she wasn't in her chair.

"This was so important to me, because I had the joy of watching her watch me come up the steps to the porch, radiating her beatific smile at me. It was what I thought about when I was away, what I looked forward to as I drove up from Detroit. Because after that, when I had to deal with Julie – my wife's name was Marja Jussila but I called her Julie – it was just hell. I think somehow she blamed me, if not for Marla's situation, then for not doing anything about it. And for leaving her alone with the child.

"Anyway, as I climbed the steps, I had this feeling of dread. When I opened the door, I heard Julie wailing. I followed the sound to the kitchen where I found her pacing around the breakfast table. She was holding Marla to her chest, her little arms limp by her side. I watched for maybe two minutes, wondering what I should do. Julie just kept walking around the table screaming. I had no idea how long that had been going on. Finally I stepped in front of her and tried to take the child from her. She screamed louder and reached up and raked my face with her nails. If I hadn't pulled back, I would have lost an eye."

Al stopped speaking. He looked down at his plate and then back up at Francie. At that point the waitress returned to our table. She'd had the sense not to stay but didn't want to ignore them. Al switched gears instantly. He told the woman that he wanted the remainder of his meal packed up to go, if that was all right – she said it was – and he wanted the chocolate volcano cake and a cup of coffee. He looked over at Francie and raised his eyebrows as if to check if that was all right with her, and she gave him a nod of assent.

"I'll finish the clam chowder now," he declared.

"But it's cold," the waitress protested. "Let me get you a fresh cup."

"No, thank you," he said. "I lived on airline food for more of thirty-three years. This is delicious to me." He reached for the cup and resumed his consumption of the chowder, again unhurried. There wasn't much left, so by the time he had finished, the waitress was back with his dessert and coffee. Al looked very pleased. He picked up his fork and started to attack the dessert but then stopped and laid the fork on the plate. He picked up the story again, but this time the edge was gone from his voice, replaced with a get-the-job-done resignation sound to it.

"I didn't realize how badly she had scratched me until I felt the blood running into my collar. As I left the room, she resumed her pacing and wailing. I went upstairs, saw the damage that had been done to my face and cleaned myself up as best as I could. I know this may sound strange, even premeditated, and I guess it was. But I had gotten from one of our stewards a syringe with enough Seconal to knock Julie off her feet. I went back downstairs and positioned myself so that when she made her circuit and had her back to me, I could shoot her in her arm.

"And that's what I did. She let out a louder holler but didn't realize what had happened. She probably couldn't have done anything if she had. She continued her pacing for another minute, maybe two as I stood off to the side. Then suddenly her wailing stopped, and I saw her fighting to keep her eyelids open. I moved in behind her and caught my wife and daughter as Julie collapsed.

"As I took our baby from her mother's arms, I could feel that she was cold and stiff. This would have been going on for maybe six hours, I later calculated. I laid her gently on the breakfast table, and then carried Julie up to our bedroom. I pulled back the covers, put her down on the bed, and then covered her again. I anticipated that I had at least four hours before she would wake up, and it could be longer, considering the fatigue she must have experienced since I didn't know when."

Al took a deep breath and released it. He took a sip of coffee and then a bite of the cake. His face again expressed his appreciation for this sojourn, despite its underlying reason. "Chocolate and raspberry," he murmured, "Quite delicious."

Francie was fascinated at his ability to flip in and out of the tragic story he was telling, both in words and feelings. There was nothing she thought to say except, "I'm glad you like it," and let him resume when he was ready. That was two bites and a sip of coffee later.

He cleared his throat. "I went back downstairs and wrapped Marla in a blanket. She was so light, I could carry her under my arm without any effort. As I was leaving through the front door, I spied her Raggedy Ann doll on the porch beside her rocking chair. I grabbed it and put them both carefully in the trunk of my car. Then I drove to a fishing hut I had on a small lake about forty miles away. It was rustic, but there was electricity, and it had a freezer. I put Marla in the bottom of the freezer along with her doll and put back the frozen supplies back on top of her. I didn't expect anyone to know about, let alone check, the place.

"Then I drove home. I checked on Julie. She was still out, and would likely be for another few hours. I sat on the edge of the bed, going over in my mind the plan that I had worked out months earlier. Back then I had had a premonition that Julie would go over the edge. From the scant literature on the subject at that time, I figured that after she woke up, she would be non compos and probably mute. My plan depended on it. I went downstairs and called the police.

"They came quickly when I gave them my story. I told them that when I had gotten home from my flight, I found my wife hysterical. She said our daughter had disappeared from her rocking chair, that she must have been kidnapped. I told her I wanted to call the police, but she insisted that I wait, in case they called with a ransom demand and threatened to kill her if we called the police. I told them that I had driven around the area to see if I could see anything, I didn't know what. I had to do something, I told them. When I came back after maybe two hours and told her it was time to call the police she attacked me. I had slapped her, not hard, and she had simply collapsed. I had brought her upstairs."

Al gave himself a breath and finished his dessert though Francie didn't know if he tasted it. The waitress came over to remove the plate and refill his coffee cup.

"The police had no reason to doubt my story, and when Julie came to, she wouldn't – or couldn't – speak. The police asked her questions and she just looked at them blankly. I had her institutionalized because she couldn't or wouldn't take care of herself. Again my job requiring me to be out of town half the month was a blessing. It took me away from the scene of the tragedy, and the loss of these two human beings I had loved so much. In truth, Julie had ceased to be a real person, as I say, six months earlier, and the baby, well, I knew she was never long for this world.

"What I mean to say is that I wasn't suffering from shock. It hadn't all happened suddenly. Thank goodness, because I wouldn't have known what to do. But my plan worked. After six weeks, just before I was flying to San Francisco, I went back to the fishing shack and packed my dear little daughter in a large suitcase. She was sheathed in plastic and surrounded with dry ice and then more plastic wrapping. She was such a little thing, the suitcase didn't weigh much. And back then, they didn't check luggage, especially the pilots'.

"I picked up the suitcase in California and drove to Carmel. It was the first week of July, the weather was miserable and wet, but before the tourists would arrive anyway, I walked into Point Lobos before dawn. I found a special spot that seemed away from anywhere that people would be walking, and dug a hole, maybe three feet deep. I'd packed a shovel in the suitcase. I stripped off all of the plastic and put my baby in the hole, with her Raggedy Ann in her arms. I covered her carefully with earth and then rock and more earth, and then leaves and sticks so it wouldn't be noticeable.

"And that was it. I came down to Carmel on a lot of my lay-overs and would walk through Point Lobos. Nearby to where she was buried, but never off the paths. I visited Julie every time I came home but she didn't seem to even recognize me. Two years later she died. There didn't seem to be a physical cause. The doctor said he would write "natural causes" on the death certificate, but she really died of a broken heart. There was no reason for me to remain in Michigan anymore, so I sold the house, and got an apartment in Burlingame.

"Then, nearly thirty years ago now, when I was sixty, I was forced to retire. I didn't need to be near the airport. I moved down here to Monterey, bought a little house, and worked as a flight instructor. I didn't need the money; I just wanted to keep my hand in. Then, as I told you, about five years ago, the stop sign. I sold the house and moved into Monterey Gardens. It's really very nice, you know. The food isn't bad. I can do whatever I want, though aside from taking walks and reading, there's not much that I want to do."

He smiled broadly at her. "This was a real treat, I must say."

*   *   *   *   *

Fast-forward a month or so and it was two days before Francie's scheduled court appearance over the Ranger Postelle ticket. She called Larry Kelb, the fellow who was ostensibly in charge of all the California State Parks Rangers in the area. He knew Francie from some Pt. Lobos preservation meetings. She asked if it made sense to him that she and his person had to waste time in this hearing. There was that marvelous pause that she'd heard all too many times when someone is considering whether or not to tell the truth. Oh, she didn't mean lie, necessarily, but not tell the whole truth. In this case, he started off with the facts.

"I asked her about it, if it was necessary to prosecute, and she seemed quite certain that it was. She said you could have just paid the ticket. You could have, and avoided all this."

"Uh-huh," she told Kelb. Officials who backed up their people "just because" were most irksome to her. "Let me ask, have you have trouble with her before?"

There was a brief silence and then, "What do you mean?"

"I mean does she write a lot of tickets? Does she have trouble with authority? Have you had complaints about her in the past? Has she ever used her gun?" They both could hear Francie's temperature rising as she got to the end of her questions, and only one of them could control it. More quietly she said, "Larry, I can't be the first person who's had trouble with her."

It wasn't a question, and that's why maybe he thought he didn't have to answer it. "Was there anything else, Ms. LeVillard?"

It was a lob, one of those questions that invited a million possible responses, but she rejected the flowery ones and settled for, "Not at this time," and she put an unmistakable edge in it. He needed to learn a lesson, and she gave him some worry.

And he got it, if by proxy. The hearing was set for eleven, and Francie and her accuser sat across from each other at the persecution – she didn't call it that out loud – and the defense tables. If you've ever been to traffic court, this was like that, except maybe a slightly higher level. When they had called the case, Ranger Zina Postelle's leather belt, riding up and down in the area where most people have a waist, called out its stress, the sound filling the otherwise hallowed halls of the courtroom.

Francie confessed to Lolly later that she did have to stifle a giggle as the ranger approached the arena where they were to do battle. She was thinking about Arlo Guthrie's tale in "Alice's Restaurant" when he told about being with the dangerous criminals there on the Group W bench, because he had once been arrested for littering. It felt like that.

If she didn't giggle, she did smile pleasantly in the direction of the judge in his elevated position, but it was for naught. He was bored as anyone could be and was shuffling through his paperwork. Her smile was because she had received a call from a courthouse friend shortly after her useless conversation with Ranger Boss Kelb, telling her that she should be aware that the judge was trying to finish up early this day – it was a Friday – so he could beat the traffic and get up to his home in Arnold in the Stanislaus National Forest, some seventy miles southwest of Sacramento. It was a nice spot but the drive could be arduous, especially on a Friday.

Francie made good use of the information. First she saw that hers was the last case on the docket. No doubt his honor expected to hit the road before noon. He couldn't have been pleased when he saw her arrive and soundly deposit five books on the defendants table. Of course they were law books. They were loud and they have that unique appearance of old thinking.

What he didn't see, but later heard...well, we'll get to

that in due course. As was pro forma, the bailiff read the jacket, claiming on this date at this time, Francie LeVillard, the defendant, had violated such and such sections of California code about having a dog off the leash in a state park. Then the bailiff called Ranger Postelle who got up, her leather complaining futilely, and went to the witness box where, instead of taking her seat, pivoted in a practiced manner and stood before the chair. The bailiff held up a Bible and in just a matter of twenty seconds, she had sworn to tell the truth, lying her way to the stand.

The judge asked her to tell the court – that was him, the bailiff, the stenographer, and Francie; there was no one in the gallery – what had happened. The ranger cleared her throat and told her story, how Francie was observed to be with a dog off a leash where dogs were required to be on a leash. She looked up at the judge and then added, "Sir, I should also like to put on the record that the defendant was surly and uncooperative."

"I suppose you encounter that regularly, given the circumstances," the judge commented.

Ranger Postelle shrugged. "It happens sometimes, your honor, but the good citizens own up to their crimes pretty quick."

"And Miss, uh, LeVillard, didn't admit her guilt?"

"No sir , in fact she refused to show her identification, and it was only after some persuasion that she even gave me her name and address."

"I see," said the judge, and he probably did. He'd had all sorts in his courtroom, and at such times must have wondered if being a judge was such a good thing. Other times he knew it wasn't. "All right, officer, is there anything else?"

No there wasn't, so she was allowed to return, noisily, to her table.

"Miss, uh, LeVillard?" the judge said, looking in Francie's direction, and then with a jerk of his head indicated that she should go to the witness box. Francie declined the temptation to explain that her name didn't have an "uh" in it. She didn't want him to know yet just how much trouble he was going to have with her. Before she went forward, she ostentatiously placed the books side by side in front of her table, looked up, smiled politely, and walked over to the witness box where she was to be sworn in.

When the bailiff put the Bible in front of her, she just looked at him. "Put your right hand on the Bible," he said, wondering if she was some kind of idiot for needing to be told that.

"I don't use a Bible," she told him.

"But you have to be sworn in," the bailiff said, awakening from his normal stupor.

"No, actually, I don't." she walked past him back to the table and picked up the first law book. She opened it to the page where she had put in a book mark and, noting the section, read the piece that said people don't have to be sworn in using a Bible. Then she closed the book, put it back on the table, and returned to the spot she'd left in front of the witness stand. The bailiff was on the confused side of nonplused and looked up at the judge whose own rote had been disrupted.

The judge peered hard at Francie. Then he instructed the bailiff to administer the oath without the Bible. Still holding the Bible out to her, he read the oath and asked if she swore to it, so help her God.

"No," she said. Then added, "I don't believe in God, not the one you're talking about. I don't adhere to any religion, in fact, so I can't ask for help from your God. That would be hypocritical."

By now alarms were ringing in the heads of the three courtroom enemies – the stenographer was doing her best not to laugh – and the peace was threatened. The judge wasn't happy. He looked from her to the books on the defense table, each of them with book marks sticking out of the top.

"It's part of the code, your honor," Francie told him sincerely, and with that she returned to the table, picked up the second book, and read the appropriate section that was designed to protect atheists and others from God knows what. "I say that because when it's time to recite the pledge of allegiance, I continue to say "under god" but I do it with a small g, as a gesture of respect but not directed at a particular religion."

She returned to her post before the witness box. The bailiff's eyes indicated that he didn't really under-stand what she had said so he shifted them back up to the judge. The judge had understood. "Do you swear that you will tell the truth, Miss Villard?"

"LeVillard, your honor, and I will certainly tell the truth...the whole truth," she added with emphasis, resisting the urge to make a dramatic pivot toward the ranger.

The judge just wanted to keep things moving. "All right, all right, you're sworn in. Sit down."

She did, and looked up at him expectantly and cheerfully.

He didn't like that but had to swallow it. What, complain that she was being gracious? She didn't think so. Not with a stenographer recording his every word.

"Why don't you tell us in your words what happened?" He couldn't help himself; he looked down at his watch. "Be concise, if you would."

"Of course your honor," she said willingly, and then she launched into an account of the events of that day. She began with who she was and how her work as a consulting detective had put her in contact with a great many interesting people and situations. She mentioned several curious occurrences in her career and would have gone on, except that after these first ten minutes, the judge thought she could "Take us to the event at issue."

"Yessir," she said but didn't, diverting ever so slightly from explaining why she had gone on the walk; that is, to begin making notes for a novel. She could have explained her intentions – the path to the Carmel River is embedded with the best – in a minute, but she took five, elaborating on the value of taking real life events and putting them into fiction because that format appealed to a larger market.

The judge cleared his throat.

Francie smiled again and then delivered a near-verbatim account of the confrontation with Ranger Postelle. She could tell from his body language and his eyes that his mind had already gone to the Sierra, or at least was on its way. So she wasn't surprised when, after she had finished, he remarked that he didn't see much difference between her testimony and Ranger Postelle's.

"First, your honor, I would like the court to note that nothing I said to her could reasonably be construed as 'uncooperative' or 'surly.' Don't you agree?"

He looked at her sternly, and then relented. "I don't think you were out of bounds, Miss LeVillard."

"Thank you, your honor." She looked pointedly at Ranger Postelle, who looked just that much smaller.

"Anything else?" the judge asked as he picked up his gavel.

"Why yes, your honor," she replied, her voice tinged with surprise that he could ever imagine he was getting even an inch closer to his cabin.

"Oh," he said. "What else?"

"Your honor, surely you noted that the ranger never asked me about the dog."

"What should she have asked, Miss LeVillard?"

She smiled brightly and said, "If it was mine."

The judge rumbled, "It doesn't matter if you are the owner, only that you failed to have the dog on the leash."

"But your honor, I not only don't own a dog, I wasn't

walking someone else's dog."

That caught his attention. "Well, whose dog was it?" He was somewhere between confusion and annoyance as this simplest of cases was delaying his departure. His eyes went from Francie to Ranger Postelle and back to Francie.

"I haven't any idea whose dog it was, or is," Francie said evenly. Then told him, "That's why I resisted when asked for my identification."

That got him. And then she said, "And to give you the whole truth, the only reason why I didn't refuse to tell her my name was because I thought she could become – how do I say this politely? – unhinged."

Before the judge could say anything, the ranger was on her feet, red-faced and furious. Francie pointed at her. "You see, that's the way she looked when she ran down the path at me to give me a ticket for walking a dog off a leash. There she was with her gun and her mace, and she was all getting ready to handcuff me. Just look at her," Francie told the judge. "What would you have done?"

The judge cleared his throat. "Ranger Postelle, maybe you should explain to the court – from there, from there – how it is that you issued the ticket without determining that this woman was actually with the dog."

Ranger Postelle looked first at the judge, then at Francie, then back at the judge. Suddenly she stopped her hyperventilating, as if an idea suddenly occurred to her, continued in measured tones said, "I did ask her if it was her dog, your honor, and she said it wasn't but she was walking it for a friend. She also acknowledged knowing about the leash law, but said she didn't think it mattered to her."

The judge looked back down at Francie in the witness box. She shifted her gaze from the ranger to the judge. He asked her, "Well, Miss LeVillard?"

"Indeed your honor, it seems we have come to something of an impasse."

"Yes we have. And pray tell, why should I believe you over a sworn enforcer of California's rules and regulations as regards to our state parks?"

"Because I have proof that she is lying?" she asked lightly.

"You have proof?" the judge asked skeptically.

She was looking at him, so she only heard the scoff from the direction of the persecutor's table. "Yes sir, I do."

"A witness, perhaps? The dog?"

That brought some laughter from the bailiff and an over-loud guffaw from Ranger Postelle.

She waited until he was finished reveling in his audience's appreciation. "A recording, your honor."

"A recording? A recording of what?"

"A recording of the entire time around this unfortunate confrontation."

"You have a recording? How is it that you have a recording, Miss LeVillard?"

"Your honor will recall that I explained that I was

making notes for a novel that morning..."

"I recall."

She could hear his energy drop. He could smell a problem by now. "I carry a small Olympus digital recorder in my pocket to capture my thoughts on occasion. This was one such occasion."

The ranger rose again from her chair, protesting, "Your honor, I didn't know about any recording device. She never told me she was recording me. That's illegal."

"Aha," Francie said, holding up her finger to make a point. In a flash she was out of the witness chair and back at the defense table, leafing through the third book until she came to her bookmark. With a confident smile, she walked back to the witness stand, and standing before the chair as if she was delivering a Shakespearian monologue, she read the section of a United States Supreme Court ruling on incidental recordings. Then she said, "This was clarified two years ago in a case involving the use of a closed circuit security camera in a shopping mall that was used to convict a robber. I have that decision in another volume, your honor," she reported, pointing toward the desk.

He shook his head. "I'm aware of the ruling, Miss LeVillard, but I am not clear that your situation is applicable."

"Then let me play the recording for you, your honor, and I think you will be persuaded that I have told the truth, the whole truth."

"Your honor," the ranger whined, "this can't be right.

People can't go around bugging people."

"Hah!" Francie told her, "I was legitimately recording and you came up to me. I wasn't bugging you. And," Francie pointed at her defense library, "I can cite two decisions – unanimous decisions – that say recordings in progress without outer-directed intent do not have to be revealed unless there is a specific question of their use posed by a legitimate authority."

The judge didn't know if he was madder at her or the ranger. "I presume that you have the recording with you, Miss LeVillard?"

"Right again, your honor," she told him cheerfully, as she pulled the device out of her pocket and held it up for him to see. "Right here. Want to hear it?"

The judge grimaced. "Yes, I suppose we should hear it."

"Well yes," Francie agreed. "I mean, until you hear it, judge, it's her word against mine."

He waved away more words and said, "Just play it."

And play it she did. She started it about a minute before the dog came up to her. They could hear her talking about a scene she was describing in her novel. It happened to be a courtroom scene in a murder case. Then there was Francie saying nice things to the dog, how handsome he was, and what a good dog, and sorry she didn't have a biscuit. That was followed by about ten seconds of her thinking – silence on the recording, except for the waves not far away – and then the herd of elephants.

When the ranger's voice sounded in clarion fashion

from the recording, Francie raised her eyebrows and pointed with her other hand toward the device, to bring this part to the judge's attention, thought it wasn't necessary to do so. Ever so slowly, the blade came down on the neck of the ranger. When their confrontation had been concluded, Francie had not been in the mood for thinking about her novel but she had forgotten to turn off the recorder. When the salient facts had been reported, she let it play for a good twenty seconds and then turned it off.

Francie's faux cheerfulness was gone. In a clear, somewhat cold but very serious voice she said, "Your honor, I don't know if this woman has problems with me alone for reasons I can't even imagine, or if other people have suffered at her hands, perhaps under similar and unreasonable circumstances. But I ask you now for my immediate vindication in this matter."

The judge looked from Francie to the ranger, now slouched in her chair, looking into her lap. Then he looked at Francie with a sense of respect, perhaps, or at least there was a look on his face that indicated he thought that she had used the court well. He lifted his gavel and brought it down on his desk. "All charges in this matter are dropped. You are fully exonerated. And I will add this note, Miss LeVillard. The court appreciates the time and effort you put into righting what could have been a wrong."

"Thank you, your honor." her cheerfulness restored, she asked, "May I go now?"

The judge gestured toward the door. "You are free to go."

Without looking anywhere near the ranger, she went

to the defense table, pulled her books together, waved goodbye at the stenographer who, fingers poised over her machine, smiled at her and nodded her head several times. Then she turned and walked up the aisle toward the door.

*   *   *   *   *

Francie drove over to the Monterey Gardens. It was perhaps the sixth time that she had visited with Cap'n Al. They had become friends, of sorts, and she had even persuaded him to call her Francie. He liked that. Mostly they talked about the places he'd visited around the world as an international pilot, and about books he'd read. They didn't discuss his daughter or his wife. They didn't go back to the Fishwife either; not after she told him she thought it had gone downhill and they could do better. Instead, she took him to different restaurants around The Peninsula that she thought would give him pleasure.

The last time she had visited, about a week earlier, she had come bearing gifts, of sorts. She had seen Lolly, who had given Francie the two plastic squares that had been the eyes in the Raggedy Ann doll which Al had buried with his daughter. Francie and Al were sitting on the ledge of the fish pond – it was where they usually started out their time together – and she held her hand out and opened it up to him.

A whimper erupted involuntarily from his throat, from his heart. He picked them up carefully and squeezed them tightly in his age-stained hand, trying to keep the tears back. He finally had to lessen his grasp, and the tears flowed. Francie might have tried to soothe him, but she sensed that he needed to let go what he had been holding back for so many years. He was a man, a World War II veteran, and a former airline pilot – and sitting before a woman – so he didn't allow himself to cry long.

"Do you think she went to a good place?" he asked her.

Francie nodded confidently. "We can't know in this lifetime what her reason was for her short time on Earth, except that she gave great love to you and to your wife. But I think that she's been back on Earth since then, maybe more than once."

He took that in, and though she didn't know what his beliefs were in that regard, he seemed comforted with her response.

She put her hand on his, the hand that was holding the buttons, and she pushed him a little further. "I'm not a religious person. I believe that we are energy beings whose bodies carry our souls. Your daughter, from what you said, and from what Lolly Perlis and I sensed about her, was an angel who would come back in other lives to spread her love. That was her role."

He looked at her closely and then down at her hand over his. "I never really went for the church thing. Especially after losing my daughter and my wife. It didn't make sense to me that a god would do that to them, or to me. But the way you say it has some logic to it." He turned his head away and looked down at the fish in the pond. Then, in that moment, he changed emotional tracks, and he asked evenly, "Is that the same for animals, do you think?"

She had spent enough time with him by this time not to be surprised, or at any rate, too surprised, and she offered him a smile and her view. "I don't know about fish, Al, but I think most animals have souls, or something like them." And she recounted to him two news stories she'd read recently. One had to do with a rabbit who smelled smoke and woke her owner by scratching on her chest, saving the family from a fire. Another was about a llama that had saved a flock of sheep from fire."

Al took it in with great interest. "They had souls, too, didn't they?"

Francie nodded.

"What happened to the rabbit and the llama?" he asked a moment later.

She sighed. "They both died from their injuries," she admitted.

"Like my Marla and Julie," he commented, "but I don't know what good their deaths did. They didn't help me."

"Sometimes we don't know, I think. Sometimes the results are beyond our understanding."

"That sounds kind of like 'God works in mysterious ways.' I never liked that." His tone approached bitterness.

"Yes, I know," she said, patting his hand gently. "I'm sorry, I wish I had a better answer."

He smiled at her and patted her hand back. "We can't know everything, I guess. But I would rather say that I know of their goodness, which is true, than to put it on some outside force I don't even believe in."

"I like that, Al," Francie said with a grin. "Makes more sense than a lot of what's peddled today, and it gives credit where it's due."

His smile reflected appreciation and affection. "So where are you taking me to lunch today, Francie?"

"How about some place special, Al?"

"They've all been special for me, my dear," he replied in as caring a voice as she had heard from the man.

"I wish that Fresh Cream was still here. It was one of the finest restaurants, maybe in the country; it was over at Heritage Harbor. Small, elegant, excellent food, superb service. Then, I don't know what happened, but they moved over to Carmel and became something of a social bar. I stopped in once and it was loud and the service was terrible. I don't think they lasted more than a year. Too bad."

"Doesn't do us much good, does it?" Al observed. "How 'bout some place that's open?"

"Good idea," she laughed and told him, "Come on. I'll figure it out in the car." They stood and she put her arm through his as they made their way to the parking lot. Danni Arnoff knew of their pattern by now, so there was no need to check out with her again.

As they left the parking lot, Francie announced, "I have an idea."

He just smiled at her. "Knowing you, my dear Francie, I expected something would come to mind. I'll be delighted with whatever you choose. Especially today." He eased back against the seat, checked his seat belt, as pilots are wont to do, and his whole being spoke of relaxation. He wasn't surprised when driving south on Highway One she didn't turn right for Carmel-by-the-Sea or later left for Carmel Valley. Then they drove past Monastery Beach and Point Lobos.

"I thought of maybe Ventana," she said to him, "but today being Friday, I suspect that there are a lot of tourists on the road. Let's go up to the Highlands Inn."

He didn't look over at her, but just pointed his pleasure at the road ahead. Ten minutes later they were seated at a window in the Pacific's Edge. They thought briefly about eating outside at the California Market, but the sun hadn't quite cut through the clouds, and besides, from where they sat they could look out over some of the more than 550 acres of Point Lobos, and the 750 acres of underwater reserve that bordered it. And Francie had sensed that this would be a particularly important time for them, and the ritzier ambience fit the moment.

When the waiter came by with menus and a recitation of the specials of the day, Al surprised her by asking for a split of Perrier-Jouet. "You can still drive me back with a glass of champagne in you, I think," he said to my raised eyebrows.

"My pleasure," she agreed.

They enjoyed shrimp cocktail and crab cakes to start

and started on their halibut and bouillabaisse when Al put down his spoon and took up his glass. "Francie, I want us to raise our glasses..." She did so. "...to us."

"To us," she echoed, and they clinked their glasses together and sipped.

He put his glass down and then told her what was on his mind. "I know you will put up an argument, but please wait until I've explained my thinking before you do."

"I can do that," she replied, thoroughly oblivious to what he was about to say.

He began, "Over the past two months or so, since you came to tell me about finding my daughter, I have grown not only to appreciate you, but to hold you in great esteem. You are one of the rare people for whom I feel both great affection and respect."

Francie felt a need to say something but kept her promise. She put down her fork, put her hands in her lap and gave him her full attention.

"As you know from our conversations, I have no family, except in my heart. What I haven't told you is that I have saved most of what I've earned and have lived frugally. Not out of some obsession but because there was nothing I really wanted. I had always hoped that I would meet someone who could take Julie's place in my heart, but she never appeared." He cleared his throat. "Until you came into my life." He smiled, "No, I'm not going to ask you to marry me. Maybe if I was forty years younger, but no. You're off the hook."

Francie could feel moisture come to her eyes, and

was, curiously, relieved that she had committed to remain silent until he was finished. Then came the other shoe.

"Last week I met with my lawyer and filed a new will. Francie, I have left my estate, such as it is, to you. Not to be executrix, but the beneficiary. I hope that you will accept this from me, because there is no one in my life who means what you do to me. There has been no one close in sixty years."

Francie was about to speak but he held up his hand. "You know that I am not some silly old man any more than you are a gold-digger. My decision is sound. It is reasoned. It is the product of a sharp mind. Even my lawyer couldn't argue with me. I hope that you will complete my happiness by accepting my decision with a minimum of argument."

"Al, my goodness, I don't know what to say. I am quite comfortable already. I think you know that. But I could not refuse a gift such as you have described. I'm, I'm flattered. I'm honored." She sniffed. "And I'm talking now so I don't cry." And then she cried. Not long, but enough to attract the waiter to ask if there was anything wrong. Francie couldn't speak but she shook her head, and he could see her smile through her tears. She pulled a handkerchief out of her purse and cleaned herself up.

"There are a thousand things I want to say to offer my own appreciation and affection and respect, but they wouldn't capture the feelings that I have at this moment." She laughed. "Are you all right with that?"

"Good girl," he said. "Good girl."

*   *   *   *   *

A week later, having concluded a successful court hearing on behalf of another client, Francie pulled into the parking lot at Monterey Gardens. She was feeling not smug but self-satisfied. Her strategy and testimony had won the day. No wonder there was something jaunty about the way she walked the path to the main entrance. She was looking forward to sharing her victory with Al, over another special lunch, this time at Casanova in Carmel.

As she climbed the four steps to the veranda, she saw Danni Arnoff coming to meet her. Francie barely had time to read her face when the woman spoke. "Oh, Francie, I'm so sorry, we tried to reach you."

"Oh, no, please, no," Francie cried. It was all she could do to hold herself upright. Danni put her arm around her and helped Francie through the reception area to her office. She sat her down, poured her a cup of water. She pulled up another chair and sat down across from her.

"I'm sorry. It was very quick."

Francie found her voice to explain, "I had my cellphone off. I was in court." It sounded so absurd in that moment. She pulled herself together and asked, "What happened, Danni? He seemed fine, when was it, a week ago, just a week ago today."

Danni looked down at her hands and then back up at Francie. "He was tired. He made the choice to go."

Francie protested, in something of a wail, "But we

had lunch last Friday and he seemed so at peace." She stopped there because she realized the import of her words.

"He was ready to leave. You have to know that. He's been easing his way for the past couple of months...since you brought him the news of his daughter.

She looked at Francie hard, watching the emotions wash like enormous waves through her expression. "No, it wasn't your fault. You gave him closure. You gave him that peace."

"He wasn't in any pain, was he?" Francie pleaded.

Danni shook her head. "None at all. I was there. His blood pressure began to drop, and he refused intervention. He asked if you had arrived yet. The nurse told him that you were on your way, and he smiled at her and said 'Oh, good, that's good.' And then he said to me, 'Tell her, Thank you.' And then he was gone."

The tears flowed. Francie couldn't stop the sobbing. Danni came over and put her arms around her. "It was his time, Francie. He was ready to go. I don't know that I've ever seen a more peaceful transition." Danni held her until the crying stopped.

Francie was surprised at how much she was moved by Al's death. Perhaps if she had thought about it, if she had realized that he was going to be leaving sooner than later, it might not have hit her so hard. She soaked up the tears, and blew her nose. She looked at Danni and nodded her head, an indication that she was relatively all right.

"Do you want to see him?"

Francie nodded. They rose together and she took her to his room. She had never been inside before. They had always met outside on the lawn or in the lobby. It was sparse but comfortable. She was surprised that there were no personal photographs, but she also understood. And there was Al, lying on his bed. He did indeed look at peace; ready to depart, perhaps to see little Marla and Julie again, if that's the way things work. Francie leaned over and gave him a short kiss on the forehead. Her lips found that he was still warm, and she hurried to push away that thought so she wouldn't begin crying again.

She took his hand in hers. He was holding something. She turned his hand over and it opened. There were two squares of black plastic...Raggedy Ann's eyes.

*   *   *   *   *

A week later found Francie and Lolly Perlis flying over the Pacific off of Point Lobos. They were together in the back seat of Avionne, her friend Geoffrey Lucerne's Cessna Skylane. He had gotten advice from a pilot who was frequently asked to scatter ashes. It was trickier than one might think. You couldn't just pour it out the window, Geoffrey explained when she first queried him, because the ashes would blow inside the cockpit. He used a very simple device. He tied two ropes to a bag filled with the ashes. With one rope he lowered the bag out the window. When it was down below the cabin, he pulled the other rope that untied the bag to release its contents.

Anyway, that's how Marion Albert Duff ended his final flight. It was as requested in his will. He was cremated with the remains of his daughter, their ashes drifting to the ocean through 2,500 feet of sunny skies. And so his last wishes were fulfilled; part of them. As Francie explained later to Geoffrey, she would have had him join them for brunch afterwards, but she needed to speak with Lolly about something regarding the will.

When they landed at Monterey Regional Airport, Lolly and Francie drove back to The Barnyard where Lolly had parked, after driving in from Pajaro Dunes. They had a late breakfast at From Scratch, a favorite haunt of theirs, and that's where Francie told her about another part of Al's will.

"Lolly?"

"Yes, France?" she said. Lolly had no idea what she was about to say, but she knew it was important because Francie refused to say anything about it until it was the right time. They had chitchatted until their omelets and potatoes and toast were served, and then Francie had unwrapped the proverbial box.

"When I was with Cap'n Al," she began, "you know that I heaped praise on you, first because of your interest in the person whose bones were found, and second 'cause you are so dedicated and good at what you do."

Lolly stopped a forkful of eggs and crab on the way to her mouth and exclaimed, "Oh that's so nice of you, Francie. Thank you." Then the food proceeded to her mouth.

"I told him I thought you could get more done for more people if you weren't focused on criminal forensics for the DA's office."

"Yes, it's so true," she agreed. "They need such exactitude and then I spend half my time preparing testimony, driving over to the courthouse, and waiting for hours to actually give my evidence."

Francie smiled at her friend. "I had forgotten that I had spoken to him about you at apparently considerable length." She let that hang for a moment. "Then I remembered him asking why you weren't a freelancer – a consulting forensic pathologist..."

"Sort of like you?" she asked.

"Exactly."

"Well, you know how much I would love that," Lolly dreamed. "We've talked about it. All I'd need is about a hunnert grand worth of equipment and bang-zoom, I'd be on my way. Plenty of business, both for the county, and private clients. Loan me some money, Francie, and I could pay you back in a year."

"How 'bout you don't have to pay it back?"

Lolly had just put a piece of sourdough toast in her mouth and given it its first two crunches. She replayed in her mind what she had heard Francie say. She crunched slowly on the toast. Then before swallowing it she asked, "What?"

"Lolly, Al left a hundred and fifty-thousand dollars in his will designated to set you up in your own lab, and get you started until your business developed. It's not a loan. It's his way of saying thanking you."

Lolly tried to keep her mouth closed while her instinct was to gape. She hurried to finish the toast. She peered at her. "You're not kidding are you. He really did this?"

"He really did this, Lolly," Francie's smile widening to match her surprise.

"Oh my god," she managed, and tears started pouring down her face. "Oh my god," she repeated several more times. After a bit, she got herself together at the table enough to head for the ladies' room. "Hold that thought," she ordered as she left the table. In three minutes, she was back, glowing like her own personal breaking dawn. She pulled out her chair and sat down. "This is real, isn't it." It wasn't a question. Francie nodded. Lolly asked, "When can we start?"

*   *   *   *   *

Al had a considerable estate. As he had told Francie, he hadn't spent a lot, so there was a veritable fortune; in the mid-seven figures. She didn't need the money, though she appreciated what could be done with it. She parked it in various places where it could grow, safely if slowly, until appropriate opportunities presented themselves. In the back of her mind, where it had been since half-way through her television news career, was the notion that she should start an instructional center for quality broadcast journalism. That now seemed possible.

*   *   *   *   *

And finally there was this. She got a call from Larry Kelb, the local ranger chief. He told her that a letter from the judge who had conducted her hearing had given him the leverage he needed to have the state parks director transfer Zina Postelle to Death Valley.

"Oh good. She'd likely feel more at home there," Francie commented drily, and then added, "I'm not disappointed that I won't be running across her any time soon."

"I think everyone here shares your view, Francie. I'm sorry you had to go through this before we could move her out."

"It's all right," she told him automatically, but thought to herself that it wasn't all right, knowing that there had others who had suffered at the woman's hand, but then she let it go.

"By the way, if it matters," Kelb continued, "before she left, I asked what her problem was with you. She said that she had heard you testify at a Coastal Commission Hearing in favor of an abalone farmer up the coast. Apparently she had dated the guy and thought that anyone who had helped him by definition hurt her. It didn't make a lot of sense."

"Ooh, maybe they'll take her gun away?"

"They should. She was kinda scary, as you saw."

"Yep, well thanks for telling me, Larry. Maybe coffee at Katy's in Carmel some morning? On me."

"Thanks, Francie. We'll have to do it soon. This Postelle business was the last straw for me. I decided that I'd spent enough time working for the state and I put in my retirement papers. I'll be heading back home to Destin, Florida in another few weeks."

"Oh good for you," she told him. "If there's not time to meet, then I send you best of luck down there. I hear it's nice and warm there, and no fog."

Francie hung up the phone and looked out her living room window at the fog. She couldn't see the 75 feet to the bluff, but she could hear the ocean, right where it should be. She put another log on the fire, and sat down with a large mug of tea. "Why would anyone want to live anywhere else?" she asked and smiled for the answer.

The Francie LeVillard Mysteries

Flight to Nowhere

A Mystery in Two Acts by Tony Seton

This play premiered on March 10, 2013 at the Clement Hotel on Cannery Row in Monterey, California, as a fundraiser presented by the Friends of the Monterey Symphony.

Dramatis Personae

Program Host: Marcia Hayes
Stage Manager - Georgia Nevarez
Narrator - Tony Seton
Elmira Gulch Shale - Shale's wife - Betty Carpenter
Alyce Toking - Shale's secretary - Michelle Lange
Boynton Chubbs- Shale's law partner- Stancil Johnson
Kurt Kruncher - Shale's accountant - Martin Needler
Francie LeVillard - detective - Amy Treadwell
Telford "Bogie" Spivac - sheriff - Fred Lawson
Francesca – the waitress - Jean Hurd
for *The Forge* - Greg Profeta
for *1833* - Tobias Peach
for *Vesuvio* - Christian Pepe
for *Cypress Inn* - Jonathan Bagley
for *Sardine Factory* - Ted Balestreri, Jr.
Director - Marti Myszak

PROGRAM HOST welcomes the crowd, explains the contest.

ACT I - SCENE ONE

The set is very simple. Sixteen-by-eight foot risers. The scrim backdrop allows for graphics to be played behind the stage to set the scene. A table is set slightly right of center stage. Just left of the stage is a podium.

The play opens with five people at a table but with the lights not yet on them.

The NARRATOR stands behind the podium. He is wearing a Hawaiian shirt, baseball cap, and sunglasses.

The STAGE MANAGER hurries up to the podium.

STAGE MANAGER: Omigod, Omigod.

She hands the Narrator a slip of paper, and exits.

NARRATOR reads it, frowns, and addresses the audience: I've just been informed [holds up the note] that our two stars, Brad Pitt and Angelina Jolie, will not be able to be here for tonight's performance. There were apparently detained by a freak snow storm at Desert Hot Springs airport.

Again the Stage Manager hurries up to the podium.

STAGE MANAGER: Thank God, Thank God.

[She hands the Narrator a slip of paper and exits. He reads it, looks relieved, and addresses the audience.]

NARRATOR: We have less well known but equally talented actors to play their roles.

NARRATOR: Welcome to "Flight to Nowhere," an original play written for your viewing pleasure, and no doubt soon to be a major motion picture. As the story opens, the major players in our drama are seated around a table at the law offices of Chubbs & Shale. At the center of the table is Boynton Chubbs, a partner in the firm. He is in the process of reading the will of Stone Shale, whose small plane crashed in a fiery wreck in the mountains south of the Pacheco Pass two weeks earlier. To Chubbs' immediate left is Kurt Kruncher, who had been Shale's accountant. To his far left is Shale's widow, Elmira Gulch Shale. To his far right is Alyce Toking, who had been Shale's secretary. And sitting in the seat right of Chubbs is Francie LeVillard, who is a stranger to the rest of the group.

LIGHTS come up on the assembled five.

BACKDROP is the conference room at Chubbs & Shale.

CHUBBS: It is for a most regrettable reason that we are gathered here this day. We are here to read the will of Stone Shale, the husband to Elmira [he nods toward her], my partner for thirty years, Alyce, his secretary –

ALYCE: I was his Administrative Assistant, Boynton.

CHUBBS: [looking at her over the tops of his glasses]. Er-hem, yes, his um, administrative assistant.

ELMIRA: More like slut, I'd say.

ALYCE: In your ear...

CHUBBS: [distressed] Now ladies, please, this is a solemn occasion, and not a time for bickering. [He checks them both; neither is satisfied but both look away; he clears his throat and continues, looking to his immediate right] Also here is his accountant, Kurt Kruncher, and [turning the other way] and as per the request of the deceased, we are joined by Francie LeVillard.

ELMIRA: What the hell is she doing here?

CHUBBS: That will be explained in a minute, Elmira.

ELMIRA: Was she another one of his concubines?

FRANCIE: No, madame. I did not know your late husband, biblically or otherwise.

ELMIRA: So why are you here?

FRANCIE: I am here at the request of Mr. Chubbs.

KURT: What was your relationship to Mr. Shale?

CHUBBS: Kurt, I think this will become clear when I read the will. If you will allow me...[he looks both left and right and no one objects.]

CHUBBS: "I, Stone Shale, being of sound mind and body..."

ALYCE: Jeez, Boyn, won't you ever learn how to run a meeting. Maybe you can skip down to the important stuff. You know, like how much we get?

ELMIRA: I can't imagine that you will get anything. He never had to pay for it in his life.

ALYCE: What do you call the allowance he gave you? Peanuts?

ELMIRA: Well, I never...

ALYCE: Not often, that's for sure.

CHUBBS: Please, ladies, this is not a long document,

but it is required that I read it aloud and verbatim to all those named herein.

ALYCE: Yeah, but hurry it up. I really never could bear to be in the same room with that woman.

ELMIRA: You preferred a busy corner in downtown Modesto?

ALYCE: Is that where you met Stoney, Elmira?

A fuming Elmira starts to get out of her seat, her intention to get physical with Alyce. Kurt grabs her hand, and when she realizes he won't let go, she lets him gently guide her back down into her seat.

CHUBBS: [starts over] "I, Stone Shale, being of sound mind and body..."

ALYCE: [in a loud whisper] He isn't any more. [and adds] Poor thing.

CHUBBS: "...do hereby bequeath my worldly goods to all of those who have been of special importance to me in the last several decades of my life." [Alyce smiles and sits back in her chair.] "First, to my long-time partner Boynton Chubbs, I leave $100,000. Boynton can use the money. I also leave him my law library and the furniture in my office."

ELMIRA: [snickers; tosses her head in Alyce's direction] Does that include the bimbo?

ALYCE loses the smile and raises the back of her hand toward her.

CHUBBS: "To my accountant, Kurt Kruncher, I leave $10,000. He needs money, too, but he's already gotten enough from me." [Kurt grimaces; Chubbs looks back and forth] "To my loyal secretary, Alyce Toking – "

ALYCE: [through her teeth] Administrative Assistant!

CHUBBS: [plaintively, pointing at the paper] I'm just reading what's here, Alyce.

ELMIRA: Hah!

ALYCE: [boiling] You want to step outside, queen bee?

ELMIRA: Aw, poor baby, let's go meet behind your trailer when this is all over, and you have nothing!

BOTH WOMEN rise out of their chairs.

CHUBBS: [pleading] Don't you want to know how much you are to receive? [that stops them; they slowly regain their seats; He reads] "To my [skips that part; clears his throat] Alyce, I leave $250,000. She did well during her years with me. I told her how to invest and she followed my advice. This is just a token gift that I hope she appreciates."

ALYCE: [boils] Why that piker! For all I did for him... peers across Francie at the paper] Are you sure that's what it says?

CHUBBS: [nods] You'll each get a copy when the reading is completed. [continues] "And to my wife, Elmira Gulch Shale, I leave the bank accounts, our residence, all of our furnishings, the three cars, and the house in Vail, all of which I value in excess of five million dollars."

ELMIRA: What? That's all? He had more than that. I want it all. I want it all.

CHUBBS: [coughs; points to the will in front of him]

This is what is says, Elmira, but there's more.

ELMIRA: What more? Did he leave money to what's-her-name? [staring at Francie] Who is she? I want her share. I want all their shares. I put up with the sonova bitch for thirty years of marital bliss. [hisses]

KURT: For goodness sakes, Elmira, before you get upset, let's listen to how he disposes of the residue.

ELMIRA: [mollified] Oh, there is more? I knew it, I knew it. And I want it.

CHUBBS: [reads] "The residue of my estate, which should be about four million dollars, I am leaving in a trust to be administered by Francie LeVillard.

KURT looks startled. Elmira is going ballistic. Alyce is highly upset. Chubbs is none too happy.

CHUBBS: [takes advantage of the shared shock] "Ms. LeVillard is a detective, like Sherlock Holmes."

FRANCIE: I'm a consulting detective.

CHUBBS: [slightly confused but corrects] Consulting detective. [continues] "I have hired her for the specific purpose of investigating my death, which I suspect will have occurred under suspicious circumstances. My plan has always been to wait until my life got to a point where I trusted the people around me and then I would remove this codicil from my will, but since you're hearing it, I didn't get to that point. I don't know how I died, but I bet that one of you had some reason to bump me off. Shame on you."

ELMIRA: [fanning herself] I think I'm going to faint.

CHUBBS [holding up the will, continues reading]

"Puh-leeze, Elmira, pull yourself together. You can hardly be surprised at this. You married me for my money and my position in the community. That's why I had you sign the pre-nup. Remember?"

ELMIRA: [remembers] Oh...my...god. That...oh. [snaps at Chubbs] Surely that is no longer in force. There was a time limit. I remember, yes, there was a time limit.

CHUBBS: [looks at the document; surprised, looks back at her and then reads pointedly from the will] "I know you're thinking that there was a time limit and there was. Sixty years. I was thirty. I was sure that by the time I was ninety, I would be living a more peaceful life with good people around me. You'd be eighty-five. [Chubbs coughs] but again, since you're hearing this, it didn't work out that way. Too bad...for you. [pauses; stunned silence around him] "So here's the deal: In order for each of you to collect your inheritance, you first have to cooperate with Ms. LeVillard in her investigation. Only if she is convinced that you are telling her the truth will you receive what I've left to you. If she doesn't believe you, what you would have gotten will go back into the trust." [Chubbs peers over his glasses at Elmira, and reads]: "And Elmira, dear, that means everything that I left to you, including the real estate. Get it?"

ELMIRA: [erupts] He can't do that! He can't do that! [looks down at Chubbs] He can't do that, can he?

CHUBBS: [shrugs, wincing] Actually he can, and he did.

ELMIRA: But how could you let him do this? How could you? I thought you loved me.

CHUBBS: [turns red] Er, um, Elmira, you know...

ELMIRA: I know what you told me, you sleazy shyster. I bet this isn't even his real will. This is a fake will. You've got something going with this chippie here [pointing at Francie]. That's what it is [convincing herself]. I'm going to get a real lawyer and fight you with every fiber of my being. [looks to Kurt] You're with me, aren't you, Kurt?

KURT: [cringing] Of course it doesn't seem fair, Elmira, but...

ELMIRA: [stands, seething] But what, you cowardly bean-counter. [flips back] Oh, Kurt, you deserve more than a measly ten grand. I'll give you twice that if you join me.

KURT: I, uh, I...can we talk about this privately?

ELMIRA: [flips again] Privately schmivately, you worm. [turns toward Chubbs] Oh, Boynton, you know this is wrong. You should get a quarter-million. I'll make sure you get that and more, but you've got to help me.

CHUBBS: [hardening] Elmira [turns and looks both ways] and the rest of you. This will is not the document that I drew up for him.

ELMIRA: Hah, I knew it!

CHUBBS: It was drawn up by a San Francisco attorney whose firm is known for never having had a will over-turned. I received the document by courier, the day after Stone's plane went down. It is certified, and seems to be pristine in its facts.

ELMIRA: Pristine, my father's patootie. No document

is air tight. You told me that.

ALYCE starts laughing, first at Elmira and then to herself; Elmira shuts up and just watches for a while.

ELMIRA: [demands] And what's so funny, gumball?

ALYCE: [finally stops laughing] 'Cause, wicked-witch-of-the-west, I'm gonna get my money and you are not.

ELMIRA: What <u>are</u> you talking about?

ALYCE: Simple, sweetie, I'm gonna tell this [looks at Francie with curiosity] person the truth, and she's gonna know it.

ELMIRA [rises]: Yeah, and...?

ALYCE: [sneering] You wouldn't know the truth if it bit <u>your</u> patootie. [laughs again]

ELMIRA sits down again, looking a cross between defeat and conniving.

CHUBBS: And there's this last piece. "Ms. LeVillard has complete and irrevocable control over this process. She can take as long as she wants to make her determination, but from what I've heard about her, she's efficient, and the innocents among you should have your share of my estate in two weeks. But if any of you challenges this will, you will automatically be disinherited. For those of you who feel hurt, I'm sorry, but as Walter Cronkite used to say, 'And that's the way it is.'"

There is silence at the table. Chubbs, relieved, hands copies of the will to the other four people.

LIGHTS go down. The actors leave the table, three of

them taking their chairs off to the far end of stage left and putting them against the backdrop. They exit stage left.

SCENE TWO

NARRATOR: This case was a surprise for Francie. She didn't know Stone Shale though she knew of him. He was a public figure who contributed generously to the Friends of the Monterey Symphony and an ESL program for area kitchen workers. She had seen and heard him at a number of public functions but had never actually met him. Though she did nothing to promote herself, she herself got some occasional press. No doubt that was how Shale had chosen her.

Though it was not a case she would have taken if asked, Shale had made arrangements for Francie to be given sole control of the four-million-dollar trust to manage as she liked, with an annual executor's fee of $100,000. Francie didn't need the money herself, but she knew of plenty of worthy causes that could benefit from Shale's largesse. And after listening to the terms of the will, and seeing the four legatees, she was persuaded that it was a worthy – and perhaps even entertaining – case.

Her first step was to get the facts, just the facts, and for that she wanted to speak with the Monterey County Sheriff, Telford – everyone called him Bogie – Spivac. She called him after leaving the law offices and he happened to be free later that afternoon. They decided to meet for something cold.

BACKDROP of exterior *Forge in the Forest* and changes to interior shot. Lights up on Francie sitting at a table. Greg Profeta comes up to the table and greets her.

GREG: Francie LeVillard, what a great pleasure to have you here this afternoon. Will you be having dinner with us?

FRANCIE: No thank you, Greg. I'm just meeting a friend for a beer.

GREG: [snaps his fingers; Francesca rushes over] No ticket for this table, Francesca. [Francesca bows hurriedly and exits; to Francie] Please enjoy yourselves, and let me know personally if you need anything. [He bows and exits.]

A moment later in walks the Sheriff in civies. He quickly spots Francie and comes over and sits at her table. Francesca appears immediately and the two of them order Sierra Nevada ales.. By the time the Sheriff settles in and they were exchanging pleasantries, Francesca is back with the bottles, frosty glasses, and a plate of antipasto; she points in the direction of Greg off-stage, crediting him for the antipasto, and quickly departs]

SHERIFF: Good to see you, Francie. How's my favorite consulting detective?

FRANCIE: Doin' fine, Bogie, doin' fine. And how are you and the missus?

SHERIFF: [laughs] Wonderful. The divorce was finalized last month. I'm in my new place, and just enjoying the heck out of my freedom. It's like I was carrying diving weights for the past five years.

FRANCIE: Ouch. But I'm glad you're done with it.

SHERIFF: So what's this I hear you're involved in the Shale case?

FRANCIE: [shakes her head and smiles] There really are no secrets in this town.

SHERIFF: [chuckles] And that makes my job a lot easier, though you would be amazed at what different takes people have of the same story. Kinda like that Kurosawa film, *Rashomon*.

FRANCIE: Nothing surprises me anymore, and particularly with this case, where there is so much at stake for the people who are supposed to inherit. I trust you heard the details.

SHERIFF: [nods his head] You have a wasps' nest there, don't you?

FRANCIE: Sure feels like it. Bogie, tell me what you know about the accident, if that's what it was.

SHERIFF: [drinks some of his beer] It's a puzzle. No body. Very little blood in the cabin. Pilot's door open. Some tracks right at the plane like he climbed out. Flight bag, headset, maps...everything where it should be. [looks around] And there was a thermos on the floor. He was known to always bring a thermos of coffee with him, even on a short flight.

FRANCIE: Oh my goodness. Don't tell me you found something in the coffee?

SHERIFF: [surprised, then not] I don't know how you do it, Francie. You've got a sixth sense that's sharper that anyone I've seen.

FRANCIE: [smiles] I don't know. These ideas just pop up in my head. I can't remember when they've been wrong. What was in the thermos?

SHERIFF: There was about three-quarters of the coffee left. The cup had been used and replaced. But I don't think you would have gotten this part.

FRANCIE: Opiates?

SHERIFF: [taken aback; chuckles] You got part of it right. Actually all of it.

FRANCIE: [puzzled] What?

SHERIFF: [leans toward her] Two opiates - OxyContin and Norco.

FRANCIE: [jaw drops] Holy moly.

SHERIFF: You got it.

FRANCIE: Any idea on the sources?

SHERIFF: [shakes his head] The stuff is everywhere. There's so much prescription stuff, where it should be, and more on the streets, too. Plus we checked and all four of your heirs knew about the coffee, and had access to the thermos. It was on his desk for a couple of hours that morning, and all of them were in and out of the offices that day.

FRANCIE: You're not making my job any easier, Bogie.

SHERIFF: Nor mine.

FRANCIE: Anything more on the crash site?

SHERIFF: [shakes his head] Not much. The plane came down in a small meadow on a slope. It rained that evening, heavily, so there were very few traces. There wasn't enough flat space to bring in a chopper, so the rescue people had to go in on foot, through deep underbrush. They couldn't get to the site until the next day.

FRANCIE: Anything else? Any guesses? Anyone not passing the sniff test?

SHERIFF: I wouldn't hold anything back on you, Francie.

FRANCIE: I know that, Bogie.

SHERIFF: I don't like any of them, but all of them had access to the thermos. Nothing else.

LIGHTS go down.

BOTH exit.

SCENE THREE

The NARRATOR: The day after the reading of the will, a FedEx truck pulled up in front of Francie's house, with the delivery of a letter from Stone Shale sent by his San Francisco lawyer.

In the letter, Shale told her how much he appreciated her taking this investigation without even knowing him. He was presuming that she knew where the situation stood, since the letter was to be delivered the day after the will had been read. He told her that he was enclosing a certified check to cover her fees and expenses for the investigation.

The letter went on to say that he didn't know who might be responsible, but, sadly, he thought any of the four at the table were capable of murder. There were some other papers in the envelope that proved to make very interesting reading about the four suspects.

Like the sheriff, Francie was convinced that it was one of the four who stood to inherit, since no one else seemed to have a motive.

Francie spent some time on the phone, and online, unearthing some important clues.

BACKDROP is exterior of *1833* and then changes to interior.

LIGHTS rise slowly on the set

NARRATOR: Finally it was time to interview the putative suspects. Her first meeting was with Boynton Chubbs, Shale's law partner. He had suggested lunch at *1833*, his treat. Chubbs might have been anxious since when Francie arrived at her typical three minutes early, the attorney was already at the bottom of his martini glass.

Francie had seen him through the window but he had not noticed her.

FRANCIE: [walks forward and meets Tobias.] Hello, my friend. Nice to see you.

TOBIAS: You too, Francie. Howz the detective biz?

FRANCIE: [laugh] I never thought of what I do as a "biz" but it's doing fine, thank you.

TOBIAS: Don't keep him waiting. His first martini

went down like water, and he's just finished his second. He told me twice that he was to pick up the check.

FRANCIE gave him a wide smile, touched his cheek with her finger, and headed to her appointment.

CHUBBS stood when she approached, and then they both sat down.

CHUBBS: [trying to make light of the situation; chuckles lightly] I'm usually the one asking the questions, hoho, but that's your job today. Let's see how you work.

FRANCIE: [with a forced smile] I don't want to take much of your time, but let's start with your partnership arrangement. [Chubbs bristles] I understand that your partner produced the lion's share of the revenues of the firm.

CHUBBS: [clears his throat] Well, I suppose -- [stops himself] Where did you get that information?

FRANCIE: [evenly] Are you challenging it?

CHUBBS: [thought for a moment] No, no I'm not. Stone had some very wealthy clients who appreciated his work.

FRANCIE: [looks at him for a few seconds] Uh-huh. Were you aware that he was planning to end the partnership and move to Mendocino?

CHUBBS: [uncomfortable] He told me some time back that he was thinking of retiring, but I put no stock in it. He enjoyed his work. It wasn't difficult, and it enabled him to live well and contribute to the community.

FRANCIE: His departure will cause you some financial distress.

CHUBBS: [unhappy] I may have to spend less time on the golf course, if that's what you mean.

FRANCIE: [manages not to smirk] It will be tougher than that, won't it? Will you have to sell your house?

CHUBBS: [angry] Who told you that? [calmer] No, no I won't.

FRANCESCA approaches the table. Chubbs points to his glass and gives a nod. Francie smiles at the waitress and shakes her head. Chubbs cocks his head but then doesn't press the point.

FRANCIE: You were aware that your partner always carried a thermos of coffee when he went flying?

CHUBBS: Yes, I believe I was.

FRANCIE: An old green four-cup model with a red cup on top.

CHUBBS: I believe that's correct.

FRANCIE: Did you see it on his desk on the day of the crash?

CHUBBS: [shrugged] I can't say that I remember. He flew a lot, you know, and as you said, always brought the thermos. I might have seen it that day.

FRANCIE: For the record, you didn't put anything in the thermos?

CHUBBS: [affronted] Put anything...Surely you don't think...How could you think that I would hurt Stone Shale? He was my friend and partner for more than thirty years.

FRANCIE: But isn't it a fact that you would be better off by his sudden death than his dissolving the partnership? Maybe by $500,000 a year?

CHUBBS: [wary] Again, I don't know where you came up with such numbers. [holds up his hand to stop her response] I won't necessarily dispute that figure, but I think it is considerably lower than what you suggest.

FRANCIE: [just looks at him; then] And that would be for the next seven years, if I understand California partnership law. That would amount to another $3,500,000 for you if he didn't end the partnership.

CHUBBS: I don't know what you are implying. I worked hard. We both did. We never argued about our relationship.

FRANCIE: That was very generous of him.

CHUBBS: He was a fine man...a good attorney and a good friend.

FRANCIE [looks through several pages of her notes]: I think that's all I have for the moment. [She stands. He remains seated.] I hope you don't mind if I feel it necessary to call upon you again.

CHUBBS [finally stands, smiles, and offers his hand. She shakes it. He looks at her.] Did I pass the truth test?

FRANCIE smiles but doesn't say anything.

LIGHTS dim.

FRANCIE smiles and exits.

CHUBBS sits back down.

[Francesca arrives with the third martini. Chubbs swallows it down.]

SCENE FOUR

NARRATOR: Chubbs will have to wait until Francie has spoken with the others before he learns her judgment of his truthfulness. That will be in the Second Act. Meanwhile, Francie has gone to Vesuvio's for her next appointment.

BACKDROP is exterior of *Vesuvio's* and changes to interior.

LIGHTS rise.

[Francie walks in. She looks at her watch and then checks her phone for email and messages. There is nothing. She's about to sit down when Christian, the manager, spies Francie and comes to greet her. They hug and kiss on both cheeks.]

CHRISTIAN: [pleased] To what do we owe the honor of your visit, *cara mia*? You must not be alone, that would be ridiculous.

FRANCIE: You are a dear, Pep. Actually I'm waiting for someone who is fifteen minutes late.

CHRISTIAN: Outrageous. You never keep a lady waiting, even if she is a dangerous detective.

FRANCIE: You're too much. [She looks over his shoulder.] Ah, here she comes.

CHRISTIAN: [turns his head and spots Elmira Gulch Shale approaching; He turns back to Francie with a scornful look] My regrets, dear Francie. [He exits.]

ELMIRA [comes to the table, stops, looks around, eyes Francie and sits down] I don't know why you picked this place. It's so not now.

FRANCESCA arrives at the table with a bottle of water and two glasses and places them on the table and exits.

FRANCIE: [chuckles as she sits down] Not 'now'? Delicious food, great ambience. It's not only now, it's always. But you won't have to suffer long. I just have a few questions.

ELMIRA: [sniffs] The fewer the better. I have so much to do.

FRANCIE: When did you learn that your husband had been having an affair with his secretary?

ELMIRA: [startled] I'm still not sure that he did, you know, but perhaps he did. Why, I don't know, especially with that trollop.

FRANCIE: And when would that have been?

ELMIRA: What?

FRANCIE: [cool] If you make an effort to follow me, this will take much less time.

ELMIRA: Yes, oh, then let me say, about a week before he crashed his plane.

FRANCIE: Is that how you describe it? That he crashed the plane? Not that he died in it?

ELMIRA: Well of course he died in it, Miss, Miss – [Francie doesn't help her; she continues] because it crashed.

FRANCIE: Did you go to his office that morning?

ELMIRA: The morning that it happened? [Francie nods] Let's see, I don't think so, but maybe I did.

FRANCIE: Did you notice his thermos on his desk?

ELMIRA: That ugly old green thing. I told him to get rid of it years ago.

FRANCIE: But apparently he hadn't, since it was found in the plane.

ELMIRA: So I was told. What difference does it make?

FRANCIE: [ignores the question] Did you put any-thing in his coffee, into the thermos?

ELMIRA: [sharpens up] Put anything into – certainly not. [huffing] I can't imagine why you would ask such a question.

FRANCIE: Do you have access to any opiates?

ELMIRA: [sharp and tight] I resent that question. [Francie just looks at her. Finally Elmira tilts her head back and looks down her nose] As a matter of fact, my doctor prescribed some medicine for me when I hurt my back, skiing.

FRANCIE: What kind of medication was it?

ELMIRA: Oh, I don't know. Some painkiller.

FRANCIE: Do you have any of it left?

ELMIRA: I don't know, I might. I don't keep track of

those sorts of things.

LIGHTS down on set.

BOTH exit.

BACKDROP changes.

SCENE FIVE

NARRATOR: How do you say, point of diminishing returns? Francie cut it off. She went to a favorite spot, across from Point Lobos, on the edge of the meadow above the beach, just south of Ribera Road. There's a bench looking out over Carmel Bay. A great place to think. Then after an all too short respite, with a big sigh, Francie got up, walked to her car and headed for her next appointment.

BACKDROP is exterior of *Cypress Inn* and changes to interior.

LIGHTS rise slowly.

NARRATOR: Francie arrived on time and found Kurt Kruncher waiting for her at the Cypress Inn. He didn't rise. There was a cane by his leg. She made a point of looking at her watch as she sat down opposite him.

FRANCIE: I hope I'm not late.

KURT: [coolly] You know you're not.

FRANCIE: Ah. Down to business...Stone Shale said you had embezzled more than half-a million dollars from him, and it hadn't been repaid by the deadline he set for you. I'd say that was a sizeable motive for murder.

KURT: Uh-huh, and how'd I do it with this foot of mine? Was I standing on the wing and I jumped off at the right moment?

FRANCIE: How did you meet Stone Shale?

KURT: [shifts in his seat; the tone is less hostile] We were part of an aviators' group. Monthly meetings. Speakers. Lousy coffee. Good donuts.

FRANCIE: What are you going to do about the money you owe?

KURT: I repaid it all ready.

FRANCIE: [surprised] Should I ask where you came up with that much money?

KURT: No.

FRANCIE shrugs her shoulders.

KURT takes it as a cue that the interview is over and exits.

JONATHAN: [approaches her table with Francesca behind him] It's good to see you. I hope you're staying for dinner, Francie? No doubt meeting some exciting man.

FRANCIE [smiles and shakes her head] Oh, hello, Jonathan. You're looking dapper as usual. No. I have another appointment. I wish I didn't. Another time, though. Thanks.

JONATHAN and FRANCESCA leave. Francie pulls her things together, rises slowly and exits.

LIGHTS down.

BACKDROP changes.

<u>SCENE SIX</u>

NARRATOR: Francie hadn't asked how Kurt had hurt his foot so badly that he needed a cane. She already knew. He had been working on a kit plane when a strut collapsed and the engine fell, crushing his foot. No, he hadn't jumped off the wing of Shale's plane at the last minute.

Done with appointments for the rest of the day, she headed back to her home near Yankee Point. On the way she received a phone call. It was Sheriff Spivac. He was in Salinas at a CHP facility. They were bringing in the remains of Stone Shale's plane. She could come by in the morning to take a look if she wanted.

She wanted. She called her friend, Larry Davis, who is one of the foremost aviation mechanics between San Francisco and Los Angeles. Currently he was working for Del Monte Aviation at Monterey Regional Airport. Would he have an hour to check out Shale's wreck the next morning? She'd pick him up and take him back. He said sure.

BACKDROP changes to plane wreck.

NARRATOR: When they arrived and saw what little was left of the plane, Larry gave a low whistle. He walked around the burnt carcass, a jumble of bent metal, torn wires, and melted plastic. Larry peered at what there was and fiddled with a couple of bits and pieces. It didn't take long. After about fifteen minutes, he gave Francie a nod and they were done. While they were driving back to Monterey, he told her what he had found.

SCENE SEVEN

BACKDROP is exterior of *Sardine Factory* and changes to interior.

LIGHTS rise.

Francie and Alyce Toking are sitting at a booth. There are champagne glasses in front of them and a dead soldier in the ice bucket. Ted Balestreri, Jr., the manager, comes over to the table. Francesca comes in behind him.

TED: Ladies, may I bring you another bottle of champagne?

ALYCE: Thanks but no thanks. [She hands him a large bill. He takes it and leaves. Francesca does a small smiling courtesy to the audience and follows him out.] I don't usually drink this much, at least not with another woman, but I guess you had your share.

FRANCIE: Thank you, yes.

ALYCE: I know you came here for a reason. Have I told you what you wanted to know?

FRANCIE: We've covered a lot of ground.

ALYCE: I know it sounds funny, having a long affair

with Stoney and not being in love with him. I mean, I liked the guy, and I'm sure sorry he's dead 'cause the sex was great. I mean, he was a funny guy. He once put a bumpersticker on his butt that said "Are we having fun yet?"

FRANCIE: [nods] But there was a part of you that hated him. Enough to kill him, Alyce?

ALYCE: [taken somewhat aback] You mean...?

FRANCIE: About your father dying after they closed the Carmel Valley airstrip. You said it was Shale's fault, representing the area residents who forced the shut down. That was five years ago. And now I don't know if you were the one who put drugs in his coffee.

ALYCE: I sure could 've, couldn't I? I mean, I had the means, motive, and opportunity, like they say in the police shows.

LIGHTS dim.

ALYCE exits

FRANCE is slow to leave the set. She stops when she hears what the narrator says.

NARRATOR: All right, we are going to take a ten-minute intermission, but first Francie will shed all of her clothes and slip into her hot tub.

FRANCIE: [to off-stage left; annoyed] Marti, I thought you agreed to cut this part.

MARTI walks to edge of stage and shuffling through her script.

MARTI: I did. I know I did. [exasperated at not finding the bit; to Francie] Can't you fake it?

FRANCIE: Fake it? What do you mean, fake it?

MARTI: [frustrated] You know, fake it.

FRANCIE [rolls her eyes, throws her head back, and pretends to peel off her clothes; says to where MARTI is walking away] I'll need a towel.

FRANCIE slides into an empty wading pool, seeming to enjoy the warmth.

SOUND of angels singing.

LIGHTS dim to out on stage

NARRATOR: As I said, we're taking a ten-minute intermission. Each table has a ballot on it for you to fill out. You have to decide as a group. You need to answer three questions. What happened to Stone Shale? How was he dispatched? And who told Francie the truth and gets to keep their bequests?

During the intermission, you are welcome to speak with the four people of interest and to the others in act one, but please do not disturb the detective.

FRANCIE: [without opening her eyes or sitting up] Consulting detective.

NARRATOR: Consulting detective. Thank you.

END OF ACT I

*   *   *   *   *

ACT II - SCENE ONE

NARRATOR: On with the show. Welcome back to Act Two of "Flight to Nowhere." As you remember, we left you with Francie LeVillard, our favorite detective...

FRANCIE: [snappishly from set with lights dim] Consulting detective!

NARRATOR: Oh, yes, of course, consulting detective...buck naked in a hot tub on this very stage. [looks over at her] Now she's dressed and conducting a meeting of the suspects at the offices of Chubbs & Shale. Take it away, Francie.

BACKDROP is of the conference room at Chubbs & Shale.

LIGHTS rise.

[Francie is sitting in the middle this time. She has changed seats with Chubbs who is on her immediate right. Alyce is beyond him at the end. On Francie's left is Kurt and on his left is Elmira.]

FRANCIE: I will not hold you longer than necessary. I am here, per the request of Stone Shale, to report my findings to you on the matter of his death, and who among you told me the truth about what you knew. While this was not a formal investigation, you need to know that I have turned over my report to the sheriff, and he, in consultation, with the district attorney will decided what charges, if any, should be filed against those deemed to have broken the law.

KURT pushes his chair back and begins to get up: I'm not going to stick around for this nonsense. You've got nothing on me.

SHERIFF [walks on stage; to Francie]: Sorry I'm late. [he stands against the wall behind her.]

FRANCIE: For those of you who don't know, this is Sheriff Spivac. [to him] Thank you for coming, I was just getting started. [looks pointedly at Kurt who sits down and moves his chair back in to the table.]

FRANCIE: First off, let me tell you what actually occurred when Stone Shale's plane went down. It happened as you know late in the afternoon, just as it was beginning to rain. A helicopter flew over the wreckage but could see no signs of life. The next morning, there was too heavy a cloud cover for the helicopter to even get close, so a large team of sheriff's deputies and police and fire volunteers made their way on foot up the mountain side to the site of the plane crash. The ground was unstable due to the heavy rains, but they were still able to get to the wreckage by early afternoon the next day, about twenty hours after the impact.

As you already know, there was no body in the wreckage, so they fanned out and combed the ground below the crash site. If Stone Shale had somehow survived the crash, he certainly would have tried to make his way down to the road, about a mile below where he went down. They searched the area carefully but could find no trace of him. This was not surprising because of the rains, and also – I'm sorry to bring this up – because there are some large carnivores in the area, including mountain lions, coyotes, and bears. These animals, whether they found Shale, weak or dead, would probably have carried him away to their lair.

What the authorities did find was Shale's famous green thermos. It was about a quarter empty, but intact. In the coffee they found traces of opiates. In two different forms. He was not taking the drug, which meant that someone or two people, drugged his coffee. The drugs were run through a micron-spectrograph and chemically analyzed to their exact composition. These modern testing procedures are so precise as to be comparable in their exactitude to matching human DNA.

One of the samples matched a prescription given to Elmira Gulch Shale.

ELMIRA: That's impossible. We threw it out... [catches herself] I mean, I discarded what I hadn't used. I told you that, when you were interrogating me, that I wasn't sure but when I went home and checked I didn't have it anymore and I talked to my, uh... and he remembered that we had thrown it away.

FRANCIE: [looks at her for a few seconds and then turns back to the group] I'll get back to the second sample in a moment. With an expert in aircraft structure and mechanics, I looked over the wreckage. He reported that a fuel line connector that piped the gas from the wing tanks to the engine was noticeably loosened. This couldn't have happened in the crash. Someone had used a wrench to almost separate the fuel line from the engine input valve, loosening it to a point just before actual separation. It wouldn't have been noticed even in a close pre-flight inspection, but it would have come apart in flight from the normal engine vibration. Not only would fuel stop flowing into the engine but it would likely spray on top of it, causing a fire.

Only someone who was an expert with engines would know the importance of that fuel line connector and its vulnerability, should someone want to engineer a disaster. The only person among you who had that information was Kurt Kruncher.

KURT: [furious; trying to stand] Hey, you're not going to pin that on me.

FRANCIE: [evenly] I'm not trying to pin anything on anyone. I'm just reporting the facts.

KURT, still angry and grumbling, slowly sits down.

FRANCIE: You all had a motive to kill Stone Shale. Mrs. Shale, you had just learned that your husband was having an affair with his secretary.

ALYCE: Sure took her long enough. We have been – how do you say this in polite society – boinking for seven years.

ELMIRA: [to Alyce] Cheap harlot.

ALYCE: Yeah? And you were the expensive one. He and I had fun together while you just spent his money.

ELMIRA: Hah on you! Now I have his money and you don't have any fun.

FRANCIE: [warning her] Don't count on your inheritance yet, Mrs. Shale. Getting back to motive.... Mr. Kruncher, Shale had caught you embezzling money from one of his charities. He had given you two weeks to restore the funds or he would go to the police.

CHUBBS: [whistled; then under his breath to Alyce]

That certainly is a motive. [She nods]

FRANCIE: And you, Mr. Chubbs. Shale had told you that he was going to retire and move to Mendocino. That meant dissolving the partnership. That would have cost you several hundred thousand dollars a year. Whereas if he had died while the partnership was still in effect, you would have forestalled that loss by at least five years.

ELMIRA: He did it, he did it! It was his drugs.

EVERYONE stares at her. She falls silent.

FRANCIE: What do you know about the drugs, Mrs. Shale?

ELMIRA: I saw him coming out of Stone's office. He had a crumbled piece of paper in his hand. And he looked guilty, he looked really guilty.

ALL eyes shifted to Chubbs.

CHUBBS: That woman is a numbskull. She doesn't know what she's talking about. I was in and out of Stone's office all day long. I left notes on his desk. I threw things away that I didn't need...

ELMIRA: Yes, but you didn't always look guilty.

CHUBBS: [to Francie] I presume that your investigation turned up plenty of information about how neurotic this woman is.

ELMIRA: Why you...I'm not taking the rap for this alone. I know what I saw and you know what you did. [to Francie] I bet your experts tied the other drugs to him, didn't they?

FRANCIE: Actually, they did, in a way.

CHUBBS is shaken.

ELMIRA: What way?

FRANCIE: The crumbled paper you described wasn't found, but several grains of a drug were found in the carpet next to the wastebasket under his desk. The wastebasket had been thoroughly cleaned. If, as you suggest, he had carried a paper spill of an opiate into Shale's office, after emptying it into the coffee, he might have dropped the paper onto the carpet and then put it into the wastebasket or otherwise have disposed of it.

CHUBBS: [desperately] I protest this slander and innuendo. You have no evidence that I had anything to do with poisoning my dear friend and partner.

FRANCIE: I'm not saying that you poisoned him.

CHUBBS: [taken aback; confused] Well you seem to be giving credence to the ravings of this mad woman.

ELMIRA: I may be mad but I'm mad at you for killing my dear husband.

FRANCIE: I didn't say that he killed your husband.

ALYCE: [suddenly, hot] So like are you saying I did it, 'cause you've gone through the others? But in case you say I did, I didn't, so I know you don't have any proof.

FRANCIE: [smiles at Alyce] No, I'm not saying you did. You were the least likely to have killed him, now. Even though you blamed Shale for having caused your father's demise, I believe that charge dissipated over the years of your relationship.

ALYCE: [looking surprise, and somewhat grateful at Francie] Yeah, you know, that is what happened. [with growing ebullience] So, does that mean you know I told the truth? Was I the only one? Do I get to keep my inheritance?

FRANCIE: [pauses and then shakes her head] Actually, none of you will benefit from Stone Shale's death.

ALL: What? How's that? How come? Not fair.

FRANCIE: You won't because Stone Shale didn't die in the plane crash.

KURT: Yeah, so he was eaten by animals. What difference does it make?

FRANCIE: You are right that he survived the plane crash.

CHUBBS: How do you know that?

FRANCIE: I was about to explain. In my investigation, I learned that Shale had been practicing short field landings. He had gotten good at it, so good that like Alaskan bush pilots, he could put his plane down on a spot with a minimum of forward roll. That opening in the trees where the plane went down was just enough distance to put the plane down and get out of it. He never could have taken off from such a small space, but that was never his intention.

ALL: [expressions of wonder]

FRANCIE: I went up to the crash site to check out my suspicions and take some measurements. And, while the authorities did a good job of looking at the terrain below, I checked out the area above where the plane went down. I climbed about three hundred yards and arrived at the ridge line. There is an old, unused fire road up there that once provided access for emergency vehicles. Once up top, I looked for a place where someone might have hidden some transportation, and sure enough, there were some bushes pushed up in front of a rock outcropping , and behind the bushes were traces of where a bicycle had been placed.

ALL: [more expressions of wonder]

SHERIFF: (incredulous) You're saying that Stone Shale wasn't killed in the crash, Francie?

FRANCIE: [nods] That's right. He rode the bicycle down the back side of the ridge, and then along a back road to where he had parked a car. He put the bicycle into the car and drove off.

ALL: [expressions of distress, anger, astonishment]

FRANCIE: I'm not sure of this part, but all indications are that he then drove to Oakland Airport, and flew to Hawaii, using a false ID. In case the police had become as suspicious as I was.

SHERIFF: [unhappy] If you're not sure, do you have any idea where he is now?

FRANCIE: I said I wasn't sure that he had driven to Oakland Airport. I do know that he went to Kauai and was there for about a month.

ALYCE: Then where is he now?

FRANCIE: He's here. [she looks toward the narrator.] The game is up Mr. Shale.

ALL: [gasp, scream, shout]

NARRATOR: [climbs onto the corner of the stage,

takes off his cap] Good evening, every one.

Elmira swoons. Kurt and Chubbs look aghast.

ALYCE: [claps her hands together slowly] Stoney, why did you do it?

NARRATOR: [to her, gently] You seem to be the only one happy to see me alive, Alyce. I guess you did forgive me about your father. Good thing. [to Francie and the others] I could say that I just wanted to find out who my friends were, but from the fact that three of you tried to kill me, it looks like I had only one friend. I knew the coffee was drugged. I knew from the smell that something was wrong, especially with the double dose of morphine. I can't say that I was surprised about my dear wife or partner wanting me taken out of the picture. I was more valuable to them dead than alive. [to Kurt] And you. Before I confronted you about the embezzlement, I put a security camera in my hangar. It caught you in there, with the cowling off. I checked and saw what you had done to the fuel line connector. I tightened it up, and when I landed at the crash site, I loosened it again and started the fire. Then I hiked up the hill before the clouds burst, like Ms. LeVillard told you, and then biked down to a shed where I had hidden an old car. Then I drove up to Oakland and flew out to Hawaii, to lay low while the world's best detective – excuse me, consulting detective – discovered the truth, and identified you three who tried to kill me. [to Francie] You were fabulous. And of course you are still in charge of my foundation, with the six-figure salary.

FRANCIE: [smiles] No, no I'm not.

NARRATOR: But why not?

FRANCIE: I'm glad you weren't murdered, Mr. Shale, but I don't like being used, even in a good cause. Besides, I'm not sure that the authorities won't want to talk with you. Especially the FAA. They don't like faked accidents. Nor do the search and rescue people. And you – a lawyer – that wasn't a smart move on your part. [turns toward audience] Clever, maybe; certainly theatrical, but I know everyone here tonight expects better from a lawyer...than to be taken on a "Flight to Nowhere."

Lights down.

End it

About the Author

Tony Seton is a professional writer, publisher, public speaker, business and political consultant, and communications specialist. Early in his career as a broadcast journalist, he covered Watergate, six elections, and five space shots, produced Barbara Walters' news interviews, and won a handful of national awards for his business-economics coverage for ABC Network Television News. Later, he wrote and produced two award-winning public television documentaries. He has conducted over 2,500 interviews and is the author of more than 2,000 essays and a dozen books.

In 2011 he published nine books - six of his own and three for clients -- and subsequently another half-dozen. Additionally he produced a weekly "Great Lives" profile for the *Carmel Pine Cone*. He also writes a semi-monthly detective series featuring Francie LeVillard, the world's greatest consulting detective since Sherlock Holmes. The stories have been posted online at MontereyMystery.com since December of 2011.

As a political consultant, his clients have included Nancy Pelosi, Tom Campbell, and the American Nurses Association, as well as a plethora of local candidates.

Other hats he's worn include teacher, media trainer, and web designer.

When he's not working, he is flying, taking photographs, and walking on the beach....though even then he is often communicating, with other denizens of the dunes, both human and avian.

Details are at http://tonyseton.com/cv.

Other Books from Tony Seton

JUST IMAGINE – a scintillating piece of fiction that tells the tale of a man returning from Heaven with a mission to tell Earthlings that they can see auras.

MAYHEM – a contemporary novel set in Marin County, California, based on the mythic struggle between good and evil, with the author being called in to tip the tide of the titanic battle.

THE AUTOBIOGRAPHY OF JOHN DOUGH, GIGOLO – a novel about a former hedge fund manager who decides on a new path – to improve the lives of women. His clients include widows, divorcees and a gangster's moll.

SILVER LINING – a novel about a shooting on the street that brings reporter David Skye and nurse Lucy Balfour together, for what becomes excitement and romance.

THE OMEGA CRYSTAL – a page-turner of a novel about how the petro industry is sitting on crucial developments in solar power, waiting until their inventories run dry.

TRUTH BE TOLD – a novelized version of a true story about an historic civil rights case of sexual harassment against a top-50 American law school.

THE QUALITY INTERVIEW / GETTING IT RIGHT ON BOTH SIDES OF THE MIC – a guide to the art of interviewing for interviewers and interviewees of every stripe.

FROM TERROR TO TRIUMPH / THE HERMA SMITH CURTIS STORY – a true story of surviving the Nazi *anchloss* of Austria to creating a successful new life on the Monterey Peninsula.

DON'T MESS WITH THE PRESS / HOW TO WRITE, PRODUCE, AND REPORT QUALITY TELEVISION NEWS - a guide to producing broadcast journalism.

RIGHT CAR, RIGHT PRICE - a simple guide that explains how to find, price, and buy the car or truck, new or used, best suited for your individual transportation needs. *Autoweek* called it "the right stuff."

If you are interested in these books, or in having your own book written, edited, and/or published, please go online to

SetonPublishing.com.

17755525R00123

Made in the USA
Charleston, SC
27 February 2013